LOST BOYS

LOST BOYS

DARCEY ROSENBLATT

Henry Holt and Company

New York

Henry Holt and Company, *Publishers since 1866*

Henry Holt® is a registered trademark of Macmillan Publishing Group, LLC

175 Fifth Avenue, New York, NY 10010

mackids.com

Library of Congress Cataloging-in-Publication Data

Names: Rosenblatt, Darcey, author.

Title: Lost boys / Darcey Rosenblatt.

Description: First edition. | New York : Henry Holt and Company, 2017. | Summary:
In 1982 Iran, twelve-year-old Reza is more interested in music than war, but enlists
in obedience to his devout mother and soon finds himself in a prison camp in Iraq.

Identifiers: LCCN 2017017966 (print) | LCCN 2016038379 (ebook) |
ISBN 9781627797597 (Ebook) | ISBN 9781627797580 (hardback)

Subjects: LCSH: Iran-Iraq War, 1980–1988—Juvenile fiction. | CYAC: Iran-Iraq War,
1980–1988—Fiction. | Muslims—Iran—Fiction. | Soldiers—Fiction. | Dissent—Fiction. |
Prisoners of war—Fiction. | Iran—History—1979-1997—Fiction. | BISAC: JUVENILE
FICTION / Historical / Middle East. | JUVENILE FICTION / Historical / Military &
Wars. | JUVENILE FICTION / People & Places / Middle East.

Classification: LCC PZ7.1.R6724 (print) | LCC PZ7.1.R6724 Key 2017 (ebook) |
DDC [Fic]—dc23

LC record available at https://lccn.loc.gov/2017017966

Our books may be purchased in bulk for promotional, educational,
or business use. Please contact your local bookseller or the Macmillan Corporate
and Premium Sales Department at (800) 221-7945 ext. 5442 or by e-mail
at MacmillanSpecialMarkets@macmillan.com.

First edition, 2017 / Designed by Brad Mead

Printed in the United States of America by LSC Communications,
Harrisonburg, Virginia

1   3   5   7   9   10   8   6   4   2

To Mom and Dad,

who remembered I was a writer when I'd forgotten

CHAPTER ONE

SHIRAZ, IRAN · MARCH 1982

It started the morning Mother said she'd be proud to have me die.

I woke with her hand hard over my mouth, her black eyes unblinking, and her long finger at her lips signaling me to be quiet. Like a lion protecting cubs, I fumbled to shove my tape player and earphones under my pillow.

For a stupid second, I saw Dad behind her in the doorway. What was I thinking? It took a heartbeat to remember: Next week would be a year since he'd been killed.

But it was Uncle Habib! He stood behind Mother, waving his hands and making goofy faces she couldn't see.

I grinned, and Mother loosened her grip just enough for me to call out, "Unc—" but I only managed the first syllable before her hand flew back to silence me.

"No talking by the open window," she hissed. "Remember, your uncle can't travel freely." She glared at her brother, then back at me. "Get dressed and come to the kitchen."

She whirled and ushered Uncle out the door. *Tap-tap-tap.* Her heels receded down the hall. The soft *slap-slap* of his loafers followed behind. The best sound I'd heard in weeks.

Out of habit, I reached for the tape player. Every morning, first thing, I listened to at least a song or two, or sometimes three. With Uncle here, I should have jumped into my clothes, but I needed one song to face the day. One song, then I'd get up.

My hair was just the right length to cover the black headphone band that stretched from ear to ear, and it was the right color, too. If it weren't for the big gray circles over each ear, I could have worn them on the street and no one would have known. When Uncle secretly gave me the tape player for my birthday last year, he told me that in America they were making earphones so small that the listening part went right into your ear. I tried not to think about it. I knew it was wrong to want a thing so much it made your stomach ache.

Last night I'd stopped the machine at "Master Blaster (Jammin')." Stevie Wonder wrote this song about Bob Marley. Genius. In America this album was almost two years old, but I'd only had it since Uncle Habib's last visit. I'd listened to it every night for the last three weeks.

My head back on the pillow, I listened and watched the smudge of first light make the shadow of the sycamore tree dance across the ceiling. My fingers played the melody over my blanket, storing the notes in my head for later. At the chorus, the door cracked open and I stuffed the tape player and headphones behind me, ready to face Mother's fury. But it was Uncle, laughing at me.

"Find a better hiding place, Cub."

"I was going to put them in my jacket pocket."

"Too big. Too obvious. It'd be a shame to have them confiscated. Those things don't grow on trees."

"I know. I'm careful. I promise." I stood, pulling up the mattress to return the player to its normal hiding place.

"Are you really in some kind of trouble, or is Mother just being Mother?" I tried to imitate her voice. "'No talking by the open window.' What does she mean? We're on the second floor. No one can hear us down there."

"I'm fine, Cub. You know she loves the drama." He tugged my shirt. "See you dressed and pressed in a minute, yes?" Over his shoulder he added, "Hurry up. She's sending you out to get breakfast, and I'm starving."

* * *

"When did you get here?" I asked three minutes later as I skidded into the kitchen. Mother was at the sink, the early sun lighting the jagged angles of her profile. Uncle Habib leaned against the wall.

"Reza," she said, not turning around. "We do not run in this house, and is that how you greet your mother?"

I stood straight, my fists clenched behind my back. "Good morning, Mother. Are you well?"

Uncle walked over and hugged me like a bear, then held me at arm's length. "I stay away a few weeks, and you grow five centimeters. You'll be a man the next time I come."

"Not unless you stay away a few years," Mother said as she checked the tea in the big copper urn on the counter. "He's twelve."

"Almost thirteen," I said.

"You have over three months to be twelve." She dismissed my words with a wave. "If you're such a man, when are you going to learn to tuck in your shirt?"

I should have said, "When I feel like it," but today wasn't a day for argument. I retucked and stared as she turned back to the sink.

Her tight gray bun was a hand grenade at the nape of her neck. Her straight brown dress, clean and wrinkle-free. When she went out, no one would see her dress under her heavy black chador, but it still had to be perfect. With Mother, everything had to be perfect.

Steam, heavy with orange and cardamom, filled the room as she opened the spigot on the urn, filling her mug. "Your uncle arrived thirty minutes ago. We never know—government agents may have followed him. We'll go about our routine as if nothing is different. You'll go to the market."

Uncle Habib rolled his eyes.

"Can I buy *sangak*?" My mouth watered at the thought of the tangy bread fresh from the stone ovens in the market stalls.

"If you get there in time." Mother passed me a handful of rials. "Bring home eggs and cheese as well."

"I'll go with him," said Uncle.

Mother swiveled to face him, tea spilling unnoticed at her feet. "Are you out of your mind? You could have been followed, and then you go dancing on the street minutes later? Why not simply ask them to take you away—and us with you?"

"Come on, enough drama, Sameera. I told you I wasn't followed. Even in Tehran I haven't been trailed for a while. I'm not that high up in the organization. If they don't follow me in Tehran, they aren't going to come after me in sleepy Shiraz."

Shiraz had over a million people, but I kept my mouth shut. Mother didn't need any more ammunition in this fight she was picking.

Uncle reached into his bag on the table. "If it makes you feel better, Sameera, I'll wear my hat and dark glasses. Do you still have one of Babak's jackets?"

Even though she'd sold Dad's piano and guitar two weeks after he died, I knew she hadn't touched his jackets since he'd left for the front. The thought of Uncle Habib wearing one seemed right and wrong, all jumbled together in my heart.

She slammed her mug on the table, spilling more tea. "You take idiotic chances and think they affect only you. Your involvement with the mujahideen is senseless. Your mutinous group only causes trouble. It's barely been three years since the revolution. You can't expect a new government to be perfect so soon."

I slumped into a kitchen chair. This argument happened every time Uncle visited. If you listened to Mother, the regime could do no wrong, but Uncle Habib thought they'd brought us halfway to ruin. I just wanted to get to the market and buy *sangak*.

Mother's voice rose an octave. "How can I convince you? The ayatollah has a plan. Iran will be returned to greatness."

"Greatness?" barked Uncle. "Not for me, and not for you, either. Before the revolution women were finally starting to have rights, Sister. Now you fear for your life if someone sees your head uncovered."

"Wearing the veil is pious," snapped Mother. "I wear my veil to show my love for God."

She turned to me. "Reza, stop that constant tapping."

I wasn't tapping. I was playing the imaginary keyboard I carry around on my thigh. I tried not to do it in front of her, but sometimes, when I was nervous, the notes just left my fingers on their own. I shot Uncle Habib a quick smile.

Uncle's voice softened and he shook his head. "You're so bright, Sameera. Think how much better your life would have been if you had gone to . . . if Father had allowed you to go to college."

That was interesting. I'd never heard *college* and Mother's name in the same sentence before. Her face clouded.

"Father was right," she said. "It was time for women, for all of us, to return to our traditions."

"I don't want to fight with you." Uncle crossed the room and stood near her, reaching out and touching her arm. "I don't want to fight with my government, either, but this war is wrong and I need to make my voice heard."

"This is your *own* country you fight against." Mother turned away and faced the window. "We should leave things to God. God will make it right."

I couldn't believe she'd said that. She knew the leaving-things-to-God talk always made Uncle angry.

"Sameera." He put a hand on either side of his face and started pacing. "You've already lost Babak. Reza is all you have, and soon he'll be called to fight—at twelve years old."

I started to say, "Almost thirteen," but stopped when I saw the pain in Uncle's eyes.

"Our children aren't coming back from this war, Sister."

Mother turned from the window. She put a sugar cube on her tongue and sipped hot tea through it. Looking first at me, she then turned to her brother. "It would sadden me to lose my only son, Habib. But if God chooses to call him to his kingdom, as he did his father, I'd be proud to have my son die a martyr. It would be an honor for this house."

All the air was sucked from the room, and I gasped to get the last gulp. Had I heard her right?

"Sameera?" Uncle's word was like a sword—a question and an accusation.

She glanced at me and back at Uncle. "If he died in a

senseless way, I'd be heartbroken, but if my son dies in this sacred defense, I will be happy knowing he has gone to sit with God."

There's a silence you hear the second after a vase crashes to the floor or a car backfires. That silence filled the room. I looked around, expecting pictures on the wall to be crooked and dishes broken on the floor, but the earthquake was all in my head.

Uncle pulled his hat over his dark curls, opened the closet, and grabbed Dad's soft brown jacket. Without stopping to put it on, he steered me to the door. "Come on, Rez, let's go."

I stumbled down the stairs after him.

CHAPTER TWO

The minute we stepped into the street, Uncle stopped and looked at me for a long minute. He shrugged into Dad's jacket and put his hands on my shoulders. "You know she loves you, don't you?"

I tested my voice to see if it worked. It came out in a croak. "That's love?" I cleared my throat and tried again. "When I was little I thought she loved me, but since Dad died . . . and now this . . . I'm not sure anymore." I put my head down, closing my eyes so they wouldn't leak. "I've heard people talk like that, but not her." I swallowed hard. "She never would have said that if Dad were alive."

Uncle cupped his hand under my chin and brought my head up so I had to look in his eyes. The sunlight crept over the buildings on the far side of the street, warming my face.

"Listen to me well, Reza," Uncle said. "She doesn't know what she's saying. She believes her Great Leader is the right hand of God, so she follows without thinking. Her heart doesn't want you to go to war, but her head and her heart don't talk much these days."

I shrug. "I try to do what she wants me to do, be who she wants me to be, but the things that matter to me . . . she doesn't get. It's gotten so I can't even hum a tune when she's around."

"I know." He ruffled my hair, took me by the elbow, and started walking down the street. "It was hard for me, too, when we lived in the same house. I felt like she and my father disapproved of every breath I took."

I forced a small laugh. "I guess you lived through it."

"Yes, I did, Cub. Now, let's forget about it for a while, shall we? There is breakfast to be hunted."

I nodded several times, until it felt like I meant it. Looking up, I noticed two men standing on the corner, one dressed in street clothes like mine, the other in a long black coat. Were they looking at us? At the end of the street, I glanced back. The two men hadn't moved.

"Did you see those guys?" I asked Uncle Habib. "Are you sure you're safe? Mother said it was too risky for you to be out in daylight, even here."

Uncle pulled off his hat and waved it like he was clearing away smoke. "I told you she exaggerates." He ran his fingers through his hair. For the first time, I noticed a few flecks of gray, and as he brushed his hand across my shoulder, I realized we were almost the same height. "Come on. We're on a quest for *sangak* before I die of starvation. That's the real danger."

We took the shortcut through Eram Garden. The acres of roses wouldn't be in full bloom for a few months, but their sweetness wrapped around us, bringing thoughts of shorts and football and no school. The sun was shining; I tried to forget Mother's words and think about the lazy summer I hoped was on its way.

Before we could even see the stalls, the smell of cumin filled the air, reminding me of Grandmother's kitchen—close and musty. The first time I'd gone to market by myself for *sangak*, I was six. Before this crazy war with Iraq. The war that took Dad. The war with no end in sight.

Even though I'd come to the market almost every day since,

we hadn't had *sangak* in a year and a half. These days Mother said it was a luxury we didn't need.

Uncle paused. I wondered if he felt the same way I did every time I rounded this corner—the millions of colorful bolts of fabric, the women rubbing material between their fingers and haggling over price—it made you feel like you'd stepped back in time. But I pointed to the crowd of people surrounding the bakery stalls and pulled him along. We'd never get any bread if we didn't jostle our way into line.

The queue moved quickly as people hurried to get their *sangak* home before it cooled.

"*Sangak*, please," I said to the ancient old man who sat next to a big basket.

The old man spread his big hands. "I just sold my last one."

"None?"

"I'm sorry, son. We only get so much flour these days. Maybe tomorrow you'll have better luck."

"Thank you." I tried not to grumble.

"Let's try that stall," said Uncle, pointing down the alleyway. Halfway there, I heard my name and felt a soft thunk on the back of my head. Ebi was brandishing a long wrapped loaf of bread like a lightsaber.

My friendship with Ebi was sealed when we took our first

steps on the same day in our neighborhood park. Back then our mothers were friends. But when the revolution came, Ebi's mom hated being told she had to wear a veil in public. Now she and Mother hardly talked at all.

"You didn't tell me your favorite uncle was in town," Ebi said, thrusting his hand toward Uncle Habib.

"I didn't know," I said. "He just showed up this morning."

"How've you been, Ebi?" asked Uncle, taking Ebi's hand in his.

"Good. Except I'm trying to buy *sangak* or *barbari*, but they're out of it up there." He pointed over his shoulder in the direction we'd been heading. "I had to settle for this." He waved his saber in the air.

"We've just been down there," said Uncle Habib. "He's closing up shop, too. Rez, I guess we'll have to get the other stuff we need and go back."

I groaned, feeling way more disappointed than I should over a lost loaf of bread.

"How long are you in town?" asked Ebi.

"A few days. Long enough to show you both a thing or two about kicking a ball." Uncle laughed.

"You could totally teach Rez—major music geek—but I might surprise you, sir."

"You wish," I said. "The season hasn't even started yet."

"Yeah, but when we played that pickup game last week, who scored two goals?"

"And who set up those shots and two others?" I grabbed his bread and cuffed his head with it. This was the stuff we fought about all the time, the definition of our friendship. Still, somehow it worked for us; we'd rather hang out with each other than with any of our other friends.

"You had a lucky day. You'd be lost without me." Ebi punched my arm.

"Shut up," I said and punched him back.

"Enough, boys. I'll die from lack of sustenance." Uncle held his belly with both hands. "Ebi, we'll see you tomorrow for a game. Rez, we are buying eggs and cheese this minute."

As Ebi headed toward home, he turned and gave us his customary salute—he stood at attention, pointed his finger like a gun, and shot.

"He's a wild one," said Uncle.

"Yeah, I guess so."

"Is there unrest in the great duo of Reza and Ebi?" he asked.

"No. I was just thinking he and I should switch mothers. All Ebi wants to do is to join up and fight. Every time the holy men take to the streets with their megaphones—you know, *the call to arms*—he and his mom fight about it for days." I shook my head. "I don't know what I'd do if he left. I've hung out with him

15

every day of my life." I jammed my hands into my pockets, feeling the coins that wouldn't be spent on *sangak*. "He says it's our duty. I love my country and all, but . . ." I trailed off, not sure how to end the sentence.

"Some boys think war's like the movies."

"That's it! He thinks he's Clint Eastwood or Kojak." I snorted. "Back when those shows used to be on TV he watched them all the time. I bet he can't even tell you why we're fighting, but he wants to go more than anything."

We passed the pot makers, the aluminum bowls of all shapes and sizes stacked higher than my head. Two men sat pounding intricate patterns into the metal. When the banging was behind us I said, "I shouldn't talk. I try to follow the war, to know what's going on, but I really don't understand it, either."

We crossed the street to walk on the sunny side. Uncle unzipped Dad's jacket. He waited until the father and young son in front of us had moved out of hearing distance. Then in a low voice he said, "Don't blame yourself for not understanding. It's complicated, and a lot of the information is propaganda for one side or the other."

I waited as a mother and her baby passed by. "I know the basics. We're fighting over land, right? And also because we're Shiite and they're Sunni, but if you made me write an essay on that part, I'd totally fail. It just seems like it's been this way for as long as I've been alive."

"Absolutely. It's been this way as long as you've been alive and I've been alive and our fathers and grandfathers and generations back before that."

We'd reached the shop where Mother liked to get our eggs, so we bought a dozen and some fresh feta. I wanted to hear more from Uncle about the war, but I wasn't sure Uncle wanted to talk about it. We walked another block toward the apartment without saying a word. Then he started talking again, picking up his last thought as if the five minutes of silence had never happened.

"In theory it goes back to who should lead us. Back in the year 630-something, when the Prophet died, there were big arguments over who should take over. It's obviously not as simple as all that, but both sides have been shaped by the fight for so long, I'm not sure anyone can really explain it."

"It's strange," I said after a few quiet steps. "It seems like it would make the Prophet so sad to have caused such a mess. I mean, we're all Muslim, right? It just doesn't seem right."

"No, it doesn't, Cub. It absolutely doesn't." He put his arm around my shoulder. I wondered what it would be like to go back with him to Tehran. "Your mom really believes if we trust this new leader, stay with the old ways, the strict religious ways, he'll lead us out of this mess. She'd like you to believe that, too."

I glanced at Uncle, then looked down as I said, "I know it's sort of selfish, but it's hard for me to trust a guy who took away my music."

Uncle squeezed my shoulder. "It's not selfish. And it wasn't just your music that got banned. There are a lot of people—musicians, artists—who feel the same way you do."

"Is that why you joined the mujahideen?"

"That's part of it. There are—" Before he could finish, Uncle grabbed my arm lightning fast and pulled me into a sweets shop.

Fear shot through me, fast as a jackal. We were alone in the shop. Uncle peered out the window and quickly stepped back. He pushed his dark glasses up on his head.

"There are two men out there." He swore quietly. "Maybe your mother's making me paranoid, but I think I saw them in Tehran the other day."

I crept to the window. Two men stood looking up and down the street. As I watched, one went into the repair shop.

"One really tall and skinny?" I asked. "The other short with a black shirt?"

"That's them." Uncle Habib ran his hand roughly through his hair.

I moved back from the window. My breathing was shallow,

and I felt sweat right where I'd so carefully tucked in my shirt. "I thought you said . . . What do we do? You think they know where we live?"

"No." Uncle chewed on his thumbnail, his eyes on the window. "They wouldn't be out looking if they knew where I was staying. I need to think."

I looked around for an escape route. This couldn't be happening. Uncle Habib had said he was safe. Just then the shopkeeper came from the back of the store. He wiped his hands on his apron and shot us a dark look.

"Can I help you, gentlemen?"

Uncle's glance went from me to the big man. "Uh . . . no . . . sorry . . . I . . . I'm trying to avoid an old girlfriend."

The storekeeper's face brightened as he let out a low, guttural laugh. "Not another word. I've been in your shoes. I'll be in back if you decide you want to buy something."

"Thanks."

Uncle turned to me, his eyes blinking fast. He was thinking, which was better by half than the flitting fear I'd seen in his eyes before.

"Rez, I was an idiot. I can't believe they followed me here, but I'm more and more certain they did. I hate it when your mother's right." He bit his bottom lip and walked toward the back of the store.

"You head home." His eyes scanned the room. "I'll wait here for a bit, then head out. I can lose them."

I went to the window again. They were closer. The short guy pulled a picture from his pocket and walked into the hotel three doors down. I was surprised to hear myself say, "I've got a better idea. Were you wearing that shirt on the train?"

"Yeah."

"I bet they saw you coming into town but lost you before you got to our apartment. If they saw you even once, they're bound to remember this thing." I pulled at his green-and-red-striped jersey, talking fast so I wouldn't back out of the plan forming in my head. "We'll trade shirts. I'll go out. They'll think I'm you."

"No," said Uncle, shaking his head. "I know we're almost the same height now, but we don't look that much alike. I won't put you in danger."

"What danger?" I asked, bolder by the second. "*You're* in danger. If they catch me, all that'll happen is they'll realize I'm not you. If I move fast, I can take them off your trail."

Adrenaline sped me up, like a movie in fast-forward. I yanked at Dad's old jacket.

"Come on, Uncle. Our hair's close to the same." I unbuttoned my shirt. "We trade. You go out the back way and I'll go here. I'll make sure they see me, then lead them into town a few blocks. I'll move fast and lose them while you run back to the apartment."

Uncle stammered, "Rez . . . I . . . This is not . . . If anything happened to you I'd . . ."

I glanced out the window. "Nothing's going to happen. Come on. They're getting closer."

"Okay." He took off the jacket and pulled his shirt over his head. "But you have to promise to stay around plenty of people."

"Promise." I couldn't believe I was doing this. It was something Ebi would have done, not me.

"Here," he said as he buttoned my shirt. "Take the hat, too."

I shoved it on and pushed him toward the back of the store.

"See you in the apartment lobby," Uncle said as he went around the counter. "Your mother can't know what's up. If you're not back in half an hour, I'm coming to find you."

"I'll be there."

When I stepped into the street, the men were fifty feet away, showing someone the photo. Now what? Beyond trading shirts, I had nothing. Well, nothing except for the eggs and cheese. I should have given those to Uncle Habib. My heart beat hard against his shirt.

I ducked into an alley where I could watch. And panic a little.

The men headed for the sweets shop. The guy behind the

counter had bought Uncle's story, but if these two guys asked, he might talk like an eight-year-old girl.

I had to distract them. I left my hiding place and, in a stroke of unintentional genius, immediately tripped off the curb, kicking a trash can as I stumbled.

I didn't look back. I kept walking, listening. Hoping they'd seen me. I breathed in the smell of Uncle's shirt and tried to walk like him.

"Hey, wait," said one of the men behind me.

"What?" said the other.

"Look there—"

That's all I needed to hear. Uncle wasn't paranoid—these guys *were* after him. And now they were after me! I moved down the street, pretending to shake off the fall. An old Beatles song filled my head. The lyrics were some of the first English words I'd learned as a kid. *You better run for your life if you can, little girl.*

Lennon's words had never made so much sense.

CHAPTER THREE

I moved my feet in time to the song, trying to keep the fear out of my step. At the end of the block, I pulled the hat down and risked a swift glance over my shoulder. The men were still there. The street was getting more crowded.

Then the Beatles song was replaced by familiar chanting. The call to prayer drifted from the domed mosque in the middle of the city. *God is most great. God is most great.* It rolled over the rooftops and into every open window in the city. *I testify that there is no god except God. I testify that Muhammad is the messenger of God.*

This complicated things. If I didn't stop to kneel and face Mecca it would be suspicious, but if I stopped they'd catch up to me.

Come to prayer! Come to prayer!

Rounding the corner, I smiled. A throng of men in the middle of the block had spread their rugs all around the square. The crowd was big enough; I could find a place and not be easily reached. God was indeed great, and he'd answered my prayer before I'd even made it. I hurried to the far side of the square, found a spot, and rested my forehead on my knees.

From there I peered out. The two men rounded the corner and looked wildly around. The tall one nudged the other and pointed. They exchanged a few words. With their eyes still on me they settled down to pray.

"Calm down, Rez," I whispered to myself. Uncle would realize I'd stopped to pray and give me more time before he came back to find me. "Calm down, calm down." I breathed the words, making them my own prayer.

I let the traditional chant wash over me. I could hear Mother's words: "The call to prayer is an honor and a privilege. It must never be neglected." As much as Mother and I clashed, on this we agreed. This was the music I learned from. I couldn't imagine my day without these notes floating over the city. Five times every day the city stood still. I knew from school that people who followed other religions didn't do this. That was sad to me.

I lived in the prayer until my breathing slowed to normal. I weighed my options. The busiest streets were not the fastest way home, but if I angled back and took a shortcut, I could lose these guys and get home before Uncle came to find me.

I picked up the groceries as the last note drifted from the mosque above our heads. Perfect. They had to make their way through the old men folding up prayer mats and chatting. I went as fast as I could without attracting attention. I ran down one block, then crossed the street and headed into an alley. Looking back I saw no one behind me.

Yes! I'd lost them. I peeked in my bag. The eggs and cheese were intact. We'd have breakfast and—

The tall man was suddenly right in front of me. Before I could make a sound, he had me in a choke hold. The bag fell to the ground with a crunch.

"Let go," I tried to yell, but it came out more like a squeak. There was no one around to hear anyway, except the short man rounding the corner to join us. They'd tricked me. One of them must have gone around the block while the other followed behind. I was afraid I'd pee in my pants. I wanted to kick myself. I should have known better. I was not cut out for breaking rules.

While I struggled in the tall man's grip, the short one looked at me curiously. He pulled the picture from his jacket pocket. I could see it was a picture of Uncle. It was blown up until it was blurred and grainy, but it was Uncle. Not me.

"Who are you?" asked the shorter man. "What's your name?"

"My name is Re—" I caught myself. "My name is Rahim. What's going on? I didn't do anything wrong."

The tall man loosened his hold on me, but only a little.

The short one held the picture up next to my head and swore. "It's not him—it's just a kid."

The tall man let go and wheeled around to look at my face.

"We wasted all this time. I told you we shouldn't rely on the stupid shirt. Just because it's ugly doesn't mean it's the only one in the world."

"Guess so," said the other man, looking again at the picture. "But they do look a bit alike."

"I don't know what's going on, sir, but can I go? I'm supposed to get home with breakfast." It wasn't hard to sound young and pitiful. "My mom's gonna be mad."

"Get going." The big man gave me a shove, then turned to his companion. "Now what?" He slammed one fist into his open palm. "I thought we had him."

"We keep looking, I guess."

I hustled to the end of the alley, glancing inside the bag as I walked. Four of the dozen eggs were broken, but eight would still make breakfast. My heartbeat slowly went back to normal.

I couldn't wait to tell Ebi. He loved anything with a chase scene. He was going to wish he'd been me today.

When I reached the end of the block, I started singing. Not too loud, of course. A folk song Uncle had taught me—back when I was a kid. Waiting to cross the street, I even tapped out the melody with my foot.

Then, from behind me, a heavy hand took hold of my shoulder, yanked me back from the curb, and shoved me into the light post. Had the tall man come back for a second try? Worse. It was a soldier in a dark green uniform with a machine gun strapped over his chest.

"What are you doing?"

"Sir, I'm . . . I'm bringing groceries home to my family." I lifted the bag of broken eggs.

"Were you singing?"

"I . . . I was . . ." I dropped my head. How could I have been so stupid? People were taken away for singing in the streets.

The soldier lifted me by my collar until only my toes scraped the ground. "Only religious music is allowed. That didn't sound like any hymn I know."

Thinking quickly, struggling to make my voice sound sincere, I said, "I . . . I'm writing a new hymn to honor our great struggle. That's why you've never heard this tune, but . . . but I should keep my singing to the mosque." I dropped my head again. "I'll not forget."

"See that you don't." The soldier relaxed his grip. "How old are you, young man?"

"Twelve," I said. This time I wasn't even tempted to add the almost-thirteen part.

"Boys your age should join the fight." I hadn't thought of Mother's words since I'd traded places with Uncle. Now they came crashing back in this soldier's echo. "Every able-bodied man must heed the call."

"Yes, sir," I mumbled. He towered over me. My legs twitched to get away.

"Be gone now. Your mother will be waiting for that food. And watch yourself."

"Yes, sir."

I ran the remaining few blocks to the apartment. Didn't care who saw me. As I came up to the building, Uncle was halfway out the lobby door. He tugged me inside and grabbed both my arms. "What happened, Cub? I was just coming to find you."

My words tumbled out in a rush. I told him everything. Well, almost everything. The part about my singing was just plain dumb, and I wasn't sharing that with anyone, not even Ebi.

Uncle put both hands on my shoulders. "We really dodged one there, didn't we."

"But what about when you need to leave? Maybe you should stay here for a few weeks."

"That'd be nice, but I have to work, and my work is in Tehran."

"But is it safe?"

"Don't tell your mother I said this, but I was being careless. If I watch it, I'll be fine."

"Are you sure?"

Uncle gave me a gentle shove up the stairs and said, "Let's go. She's not going to be happy. It took us a long time to come back with some cheese and four broken eggs."

"And we can't even tell her why." I tried to laugh.

"No, we certainly can't." He took the bag from me and started up the stairs. I took one last look out into the empty street.

CHAPTER FOUR

As it turned out, Mother wasn't even there. She'd left a note: *I couldn't wait. My volunteer shift at the hospital is over by five. I'll be back in time to prepare dinner. The family will be here at six.*

I looked around the empty room. The sunlight sent shadows from the table legs across the room. Uncle was watching me. "What's going on in that brain, Cub?"

I shrugged. "Just thinking about how quiet the apartment is since Dad's gone. About how stupid I am for thinking she might be sorry for what she said." I walked to the window to stare down at the sidewalk below. "Maybe I should just go. Especially if Ebi goes. I couldn't stand it here on my own without him. Besides, they might make us go soon, anyway. That's what people are saying."

"I hope to God you won't be called, but as you may have noticed, I'm not in charge." He went to the cupboard and pulled out a pan for the eggs. "Rez, I wish I could take you with me. But for now, just stick it out. Remember who your mother is—where she comes from. Our father dedicated his life to religion. He was a holy man."

"I know, I know, and his father and his father before him. I come from a long line of holy, pious men." I sat down and crossed my arms. "I've heard it a million times."

"You've heard it, but unless you've lived it, it's hard to understand how much it influenced our lives, especially her life." The eggs started sizzling on the stove.

"What? You think it hasn't influenced my life?" I blurted. I didn't want to hear the same tired words from Uncle that I heard from Mother every single day. I couldn't stop my voice from getting too loud. "Before the war, all she wanted was for me to be like her father. Now all she wants is for me to go to war so she can be proud. Even if I die."

"Sorry, sorry." Uncle put the spatula down and turned toward me. "I know how hard it is to live with that pressure."

"Some of the guys at school, their parents are sending them to Europe or America so they don't have to sign up. We don't have distant family there, do we?"

"Nooo." Uncle stretched out the word, as if there should be a *but* after it.

"What?"

"Nothing. I was just trying to think." He divided the eggs between two plates, put some of the fresh feta on the side, and brought the plates to the table.

"You had an idea," I said, trying not to get excited. "I could tell. You have friends in America and in England—right?" I stood, knocking a fork to the floor. "And I have some money saved up."

"Sit down," Uncle said as he sat. "I don't think you know what you're asking. Leaving the place you've lived all your life? Going far away to a country where you don't speak the language?"

"They'd have music there." I sat but couldn't keep my hands from waving around while I talked. "I'd learn the language. I already speak a little English. It wouldn't be forever. This war has to end sometime—right? And"—I paused, choosing my words—"like I said, they'd have music there."

Uncle took a bite of his eggs and motioned for me to do the same. "I know it's tempting, but you need to think about what this would mean to your relationship with your mom. I know you're angry at her right now, but—"

"Uncle, she wants me to die." I slammed both palms onto the table with a little more force than I'd meant to. "I don't want to die for something I don't even understand."

I hadn't been this mad since the months after Dad died, but something in me was excited, too. I stared at him, saying nothing. Finally he said, "I do know people, but even a visit would be complicated. Let me think about this for a bit. Okay?"

I nodded, afraid if I spoke, the hope I held in my throat would fly away. Uncle cuffed my shoulder. "That's enough history and family stuff for one day. Let's talk about something else. I assume you haven't found anywhere else to play?"

"No. Ebi thought I could use the piano at his aunt's house, but she was afraid we'd get caught."

"What about your dad's old guitar? You played that a few times, right? Is it still around?"

I shook my head and said, "But look." I went over to Dad's bookcase and wiggled it away from the wall, reaching into my secret hiding place.

"What's this?" asked Uncle.

"I didn't want to forget how to play, so I made my own keyboard." I unfolded the long, stiff piece of paper I'd snuck from school. The keys I'd painted black were already fading from overuse. "See, I can still play and hear it in my head. It'll have to do until I can find the real thing."

I flexed my fingers and ran them across the makeshift keys. "Remember that sonata I was learning? It goes like this." I closed my eyes and hummed as my fingers reached for the keys. When I touched each piece of paper ivory, I remembered the sound from our old upright. It was like putting on a shirt that covered me from the inside out and fit perfectly.

When I finished, I looked up to see Uncle shaking his head.

"What?" I asked.

"You're amazing. You can hold an entire melody in your head. It's incredible."

I looked down at my fingers. "I thought everyone could do that."

Uncle shook his head. "No, not everyone can do that. Now, why don't you go get that fancy tape player you didn't hide very well this morning?"

I was back in a flash. But as I handed him the tape player, we heard the second call to prayer waft through the open window.

I put away my keyboard and put down the tape player. Prayer with Uncle Habib always felt different. Just the two of us felt like an oasis where God knew who I was.

CHAPTER FIVE

After prayers, Uncle pulled a tape from his bag. I held my hands clasped tight behind my back so I wouldn't grab.

"Thank you so much, Uncle."

"Don't thank me yet. You don't know if you like what I brought," he said.

"I always like what you bring. That Stevie Wonder you gave me last month? I play it every morning and every night."

He shook his head. "And your mother has no idea?"

"Nope. I'm careful."

"Good. I don't know what she'd do if she found this tape player." He stroked the plastic box lightly. "For today I brought some Mozart. I know you've heard his stuff before. Your dad liked the Sonata in C. It's probably Mozart's most popular, but I like these, especially the Sonata in B-flat."

I put the earphones on. Uncle pushed play. I pictured my keyboard. As the music began, I could hear where my fingers should be. I don't know how long I lived in the new music before Uncle gently pulled the earphones off.

"Don't be greedy. Let's try another one." He reached into his bag, then sat back on his heels, thinking.

"Do you remember 'You Worry Too Much'? It's a song by Rumi that I taught you when you were four."

"Barely," I said. "He was a religious guy, right?"

"He was religious, but he was really a poet. He was your kind of guy, Cub. Even though he died in 1273, he was all about reaching God through singing and dancing. Next time I come, I'll bring some modern interpretations. But for today I have something else. You were so happy with Charlie Parker, I brought you a contemporary of his." He handed me another tape. "I give you the amazing Mr. Thelonious Monk."

I loved the sound of the man's name even without hearing his music. Thelonious Monk—a genie from this sparkling plastic box.

"Sometimes he leaves silence where you think the notes should go," said Uncle. "He played the keys like no one before or since."

I put on the earphones again and started the tape. At first, it hurt to listen. Instead of the instruments working together in the same melody, each was dancing in its own world. But as I watched the sunlight play with the dust above the kitchen table, I realized the separate dances were moving in the same direction.

The saxophone wailed like women at funeral marches—high and sad. The sound stayed far from the melody, then as if by magic the piano jumped ahead, pulling the saxophone back into the dance. When they came together, the bass was right there waiting. The notes jumbled together, colored leaves tumbling down a stream. My face exploded in a grin. I looked at Uncle, and he was smiling, too.

"I knew you'd get it," he said loud enough for me to hear. "I can see it in your face. Some people think this is just noise, but not you."

"How can this be?" I whispered, moving one earphone back so I could hear myself talk. "There's so much going on."

"Exactly." Uncle jumped up. "And you know this jazz comes from American slavery. Picture a whole people caged—you hear that sadness? But music was their subtle rebellion, something that made them free. It's no surprise our government bans music. Music can be power to people who are struggling."

"Mother would hate it," I said, glancing at the door to her room.

"She doesn't understand it, so yes, she would probably hate it." Uncle went to the urn and opened the spigot until dark tea filled his glass.

"And I'm sorry, Reza, that she doesn't understand you. She doesn't understand the gift God's given you. I hope that sometime, somewhere, there'll be a place where you can grow your gift."

I looked at him. What kind of place could that be? Could I really go to England or America? A place where I could play music all the time? Sitting in this apartment, I couldn't imagine getting there from here.

I heard a key at the door and looked wildly at Uncle. Mother wasn't due home for hours.

I yanked the earphones off, looking for somewhere to hide the tape player, to hide myself, but it was too late. The door flew open and Mother walked in. I couldn't comprehend her and this music occupying the same space. She looked at both of us. Her face went white. A full moon against a daytime blue sky. She raised her fists on either side of her head. She looked as if she couldn't decide who to hit first.

Then in a second she stood inches from my face. She ripped the machine from my hand and threw it to the floor. The earphones flew across the room, the music dying in a crash of splintering plastic.

"You!" She turned to Uncle Habib. "Your ideas and your words of disrespect are one thing. I tolerate them because you are my brother, but when you bring this wicked noise into the house, there is no forgiving that. You have divorced yourself from God." She stared at him with her fists by her side. "Leave immediately."

"No, Mother," I wailed. "He isn't hurting—"

She wheeled on me. "Not another word from you."

"Sameera." Uncle gave Mother a cool, angry stare. "How is it God's plan to keep the boy from something he loves?" I saw the similarity, brother to sister, in their clenched jaws. "You were kept from learning what you loved. Don't do that to your son."

"Not another word from you, either." Each syllable was a hammer, striking a flat-head nail, but I thought I saw a tear she quickly brushed away. "Do you think it's easy for me, raising a child by myself? I try to teach him God's ways. I try to keep him pure. And you come to him with your rock and roll."

"Mother, it's not . . . ," I started, but stopped. This was not the time for a lesson on the difference between jazz and rock.

"You are my younger brother, Habib." She ran her hand across her face. "I thought you would have more respect."

"I respect you, Sameera. I do," pleaded Uncle. "But Reza's special, and I believe that's God given. It deserves—"

"Stop." The sound was both bark and sob. She turned her back on us. There was silence until she slowly faced Uncle. "Habib, take your belongings. And you, Reza, will not move until he has closed that door behind him."

Uncle stared at me, then at Mother. He took a step toward her. She stepped back and pointed to the apartment door. He slung his small canvas bag over his shoulder.

"Please, Mother," I tried again, but she held her palm up like she was stopping traffic.

Uncle walked over to me. He leaned close and whispered, "I'll see you soon. Keep singing. Dance when you can, Cub." He pulled his hat low and was out the door and gone. I hoped the men who'd followed me this morning were gone, too.

*　*　*

It was too late to cancel the dinner Mother had planned for Uncle. So that night the whole family gathered at the apartment. Without him it didn't feel like family to me. I sat on the window ledge, watching steam fog the glass, smelling garlic, chicken, and dates. Arms crossed, I listened to the conversation around me.

"I've been tolerant of his wild ideas and stories of rebellion," Mother said to her sisters. "But bringing blasphemous music into our home and exposing Reza is beyond what I can stand."

"Sister," said Aunt Azar. "Habib is still foolish. Give him time. He'll come back to visit next month and he'll apologize."

I caught Aunt Azar's eye, and she sent me a shadow of a smile.

Aunt Bita carried tea and a bowl brimming with nuts from the kitchen. "My neighbor's apartment was full of tapes and records," she said. "The police came in and destroyed them. They took him off for a sound beating. He didn't walk for days."

"The rules are clear," said Mother. "And this Western music is against the will of God."

The conversation droned on. My fingers drummed a slow tune on the glass, where no one could see. It was something Uncle had sung when he visited last year. Was it John Lee Hooker? I couldn't remember.

I pressed my forehead against the window. I stopped drumming and formed fists in my lap. Would I wake up one day and suddenly know God, like Mother did, or even like Father had? After that would I find a job like Father's in the city? Or would I be more like Uncle? If my destiny was the will of God, I wished it was written down somewhere in a big library, where I could go look it up.

I wanted to believe in something. I wanted to know who wrote the song in my head. I wanted to run into the night and go after Uncle.

"Reza," said Mother. "Come join our guests."

I looked into the darkness, wondering how she could even say my name when this morning she'd wished me dead, but when she asked again I did as she commanded. I'd never been out at night by myself and I wasn't going tonight. Like a good boy, I'd go to school tomorrow and the next day and all the endless days until Uncle Habib came back. But my fists stayed clenched in my pockets.

Hours after the guests were gone I lay awake. Getting up, I went to the living room and stood in front of the wastebasket that held my broken tape player. It was partly covered, but I could see the corner of cracked plastic. With one eye on the door to Mother's room, I reached through wet tea leaves and pulled out the machine. It was cracked in several places and would never work again, but it opened to my touch. On the tape, Uncle had written "Monk—the best."

After hurrying back to my room, I slipped the tape into the inside pocket of my jacket.

As expected, Ebi was jealous the next morning when I told him about my very own chase scene. He was less interested in the fight between Mother and Uncle. I didn't tell him what Mother had said.

"That must have been so cool, Maggot. I should've been there."

Maggot was a character from Ebi's favorite American movie, *The Dirty Dozen*. The first time he saw the war movie years ago he turned Maggot into my nickname.

"Who were they? Maybe they were Iraqis? They're such bastards, we need to pulverize them."

"I don't know if they were Iraqis or government goons. It's all so stupid. Did you hear Dara's older brother was killed last week? That makes eleven guys from school in the last three months." I took an orange from my lunch pail and started peeling.

"Yeah, and we owe it to them to strike back." Ebi punched an unseen target. "We need to get even." I shrugged and let him keep talking. "The clerics from the mosque are coming to school tomorrow to talk about joining up. Maybe then I can convince you and my mother."

That afternoon our whole class watched the weekly funeral

procession. Dozens of men walked solemnly down the avenue. Some carried a poster with the face and name of a dead soldier.

The first time this happened over a year ago, it seemed sad and scary. Now it happened so often, we didn't think about it much.

Ebi elbowed me in the ribs as we lined up. "Look, the girls are out today, too."

I followed his gaze. It was getting warm and my starched white button-down shirt felt clammy on the back of my neck. I glanced at the girls lined up in front of their school across the street. They must have been miserable in their dark uniforms and veils.

"Remember when we used to have those special assemblies with them?" I asked. "Back when they wore skirts and sandals."

"Yeah, can you believe we thought girls were lame then? Now this is as close to them as we get. Unless you count my cousins."

"What about your sister?" I asked.

Ebi snorted. He had an eight-year-old sister, but neither of us considered her a real girl.

"She might be the only girl you have a chance with," he teased. "You with the crooked nose and your weird stuck-out ears. But see the one just in from the end?" Ebi pointed. "I think that's Parto; she lives on our block."

"You can't tell it's her, freak," I said, squinting into the sun. "The only thing not covered are her eyes, and she's standing all the way across the street."

"Well, she has beautiful eyes. I think she might be looking at me."

While Ebi bragged about his "girl" to someone else, I stared at the slow stream of wooden boxes. Lately the men marching were getting older. Could it be that all the young guys were already at the front? Or worse—already dead?

There was no talk of the funeral march the next day when the men from the mosque came to class. My nose itched from the chalk dust we'd raised with our thorough cleaning. Now we sat, a little like soldiers, in our straight rows of desks. Our teachers stood silently in the back while the two holy men, dressed in long black robes and white turbans, walked in. Ebi, on the edge of his chair, moved one leg up and down, fast. His whole desk jiggled.

One of the men was older than the other. His long, gray beard reached to his chest. The younger man's beard was dark and scraggly around his face. He held a small wooden box under one arm.

The older one spoke in a raspy voice. "We've come to talk to you today about something that is crucial to the future of Islam—crucial to *your* future. As you know, we are engaged in an ongoing battle with Iraqi forces." His voice grew louder with every word. "We are involved in sacred defense. The terrible Iraqi government is oppressing its citizens and threatening our very existence. We must bleed the enemies of God anywhere, by any means."

I heard Uncle's voice in my head, telling me this struggle had been going on forever. I wished I knew where Uncle was. I hoped the two men who'd chased me didn't know, either. I thought about who he might know in England and America.

The cleric's steely gaze traveled each row. "We have come to ask you to join with us in this glorious struggle. Put aside your daily lives for Islam."

Several boys cheered. Ebi joined in, his fist in the air. I loved my country. I thought of the market and the city just before dark, of the mountains where we vacationed before the war. Why couldn't I raise my fist?

When the shouting died down, the old man continued, "You are all smart young men and know the danger and sacrifice are real. But you will be part of something greater than yourselves. And if you should be lucky enough to die in this

holy war, you will be dying for God. There is no better sacrifice than this."

I closed my eyes and saw Mother's face as she stood in our
kitchen.

"We are handing each of you a key." The old man's voice
reverberated against the white plaster walls.

The younger man opened the box for Arash, who sat in the
front row. Arash reached in and brought out a small gold-colored
key on a black string. The man walked down the aisle, handing
each boy a key, making his way toward me.

"This key is important. It is a holy gift, for if you join us
and are killed in this gallant battle, you will ascend to paradise.
You will live for eternity in a place full of more riches than you
can imagine; food, palaces, and beautiful women will be yours
for all time." As soon as he said the part about beautiful women,
everyone cheered again.

"Place this key around your neck and join us. If this war
goes on much longer you will all be ordered to serve, but now
you can choose to join the struggle of your own free will. Serve
your country and Hazrat Muhammad and this token will be your
key to paradise, your key to heaven."

We streamed out of the classroom. It felt like all the air had
already been used by the boys jostling down the hall. Ebi had
the black string around his neck, strutting around, holding the

key where he could see it. Two boys careened into us, waving their keys in the air.

"Ebi, Reza, when are you joining up?"

"You heard what he said about beautiful girls, didn't you? And they're all virgins."

"So they say," said Ebi. "I'm joining this month. No matter what my mother says."

"Reza, what about you?"

"I don't know." I wanted to be somewhere else. "What if they're wrong? What if heaven is hot and dusty and you have to work all the time and there aren't any girls at all?"

"That sounds like my life," laughed Ebi. "Come on, Maggot, it's gonna be great. We'll be away from our parents and school, and if we die we'll go straight to paradise."

"Maybe," I said, shoving the plastic key into my pocket. Grandma and Grandpa didn't die in the war. They weren't martyrs. Did that mean they weren't in heaven?

* * *

For a few hours homework was a distraction. I hunched over the small table, reading while Mother prepared dinner.

"I saw Ebi's mother on the way home this evening," she said once she sat down. "She mentioned that the holy men visited school today."

I stared at my plate. "Ebi wants to sign up right away."

"And you?"

"I don't know." I pushed my vegetables around. "It's not that I'm afraid. It's just that it seems like a stupid way to solve problems."

"You sound like your uncle. He left this house not a minute too soon." She waved her fork at me. "Talking is for little boys. If the battle is just, fighting is noble."

Something like a snake coiled quickly around my heart and squeezed. Just above a whisper I asked, "If I left, wouldn't it bother you to be by yourself? Or would you rather I wasn't here at all?"

"If you can be of use, I'm not afraid to live by myself."

"Maybe I should go tomorrow." I stood and dropped my plate into the sink.

"It's not that I don't want you here, Reza." Mother's voice was slightly softer, but it reminded me of gravel underfoot. "I don't want you to shrink from your duty to God and as a man."

Before I could respond, I heard footsteps in the hallway. We both turned and looked at the door. We didn't get visitors. I thought of the tapes hidden in my jacket pocket. Then my heart leaped—maybe it was Uncle, coming back to make peace.

There was a sharp *rap-rap-rap.*

I stood behind Mother as she turned the knob. A large man in a dark suit filled the doorway.

"Are you Sameera Mirzai?"

"I am," said Mother as she opened the door farther. I shifted from one foot to the other.

"My name is Bahram. I am . . . I was . . ." The man shook his head quickly, closing his eyes for a fraction of a second. "I *am* a friend of your brother, Habib."

CHAPTER SIX

There was no sound in the whole world for what seemed like minutes. "I've been sent to inform you that there was a bombing and . . ." He hung his head, closed his eyes, and took a deep breath before continuing. "He died in the hospital four hours ago."

Without thinking, I lunged for the man and grabbed his arm. "No. No. No." The same word kept coming out of my mouth. Somehow the bones in my legs dissolved. He held me to keep me from slipping to the floor. "You must be Reza," he said softly.

I stared at this man I didn't know. This man I didn't want to know or ever see again.

He led me, almost carried me, to the nearest chair and sat me down. Then he knelt so his face was right in front of mine. I stared at him, watched the tears gather and slide down his cheeks. His tears, like falling dominoes, triggered mine. He swallowed and cleared his throat twice. "He talked about you all the time. How smart you are." He lowered his voice. "How talented."

I couldn't believe I was still breathing, or that the earth hadn't tilted on its axis, throwing us into dark nothingness. My voice came out in a croak, saying the only word I knew anymore. "No. No. No."

Bahram reached for my hands and held them in his for a long moment. Mother hadn't moved, her hand still on the doorknob. Bahram stood and looked at both of us. "Habib was a great man and a great friend. Is there any way I can help you, Mrs. Mirzai? Can I wait until family comes?"

Mother said in a low voice, "We will be fine."

"Are you sure? I'd be happy to—"

"I said we would be fine." This time there was a ragged edge to her voice that made me look up and Uncle's friend take a step back.

He paused, then took a package out of the bag he had strapped across his shoulder and handed it to Mother. He knelt down again and put a hand on either side of my face. "May God be with you." As he went out the door, he said, "May God be with you both."

"No, no, no, no . . ." I pushed my whispering voice deep, where only I could hear it. I realized as his footsteps faded, I had questions. "Did he say anything? Was he in pain?" But it was too late. Bahram was gone.

I looked up at Mother. She stared in my direction for a long moment, with one tear running down her cheek, but her mouth was a tight, straight line.

I heard her walk to the sink and do the dishes. After a time she came and rested her hand lightly on the back of my head. She said, "Sitting there won't bring him back." I didn't respond. She turned and walked toward her room.

"Is he in heaven now?" I didn't realize I'd said the words out loud until Mother turned.

"I don't know. I hope so. I know, even though we may not understand, it was God's plan." My chest shuddered with another sob. "Go to sleep, son. The day will begin again tomorrow."

I watched the door close behind her. What would my world be without Uncle? He loved me for all I am and for the dreams no one else knew. A world without him made me feel like an empty bottle thrown by the side of the road. Thrown away because it was made for a reason and now that reason was gone.

I wrapped my arms around my head, trying to keep the tears in, or at least to stay quiet enough that Mother wouldn't hear. A picture of Uncle, dancing and laughing at a cousin's wedding, brought a sob that almost made me throw up.

I don't remember what happened after that. I remember crying and I remember resting my forehead on my knees that were wet from crying, but I have no idea how long I sat like this.

Eventually I pulled my head up. The apartment around me was quiet and cold; there was no noise from the street. Mother's door was still closed. I moved to the kitchen. I stood in the dark for a long time before I noticed I held the package from Uncle's friend.

All I had of Uncle fit in the palm of my hand.

Turning on the light, I fumbled with the package's string. Inside was the hat we'd both worn a few days before. Under the hat was the wallet I'd given him for his last birthday. It was worn and smooth and fit his body.

Behind an identification card and a few bills were a couple of pictures, frayed at the edges. One of me as a toddler sitting on Uncle's lap—just what I'd wished for an hour before as I huddled in the chair.

I held the photo for a long time before slipping it back into place. Taking the package into my room, I put the wallet in my jacket pocket with the Thelonious Monk tape.

*   *   *

Making things worse, my songs vanished. I couldn't even hum the rhymes he'd taught me. The circus of sound I usually carried around in my head was gone, leaving a barren field.

The family gathered a few days after we got the news. When Mother was out of the room, Aunt Azar said, "We *all* miss him, but it is hardest for you. You were his favorite."

Then she hugged me and it all came crashing in. I couldn't stop the tears. My throat closed up and my lungs searched for air. Auntie pulled me into the hall, away from the others, and hugged me tight.

"It's all right, my boy. It's all right to be sad. You honor him with your sadness."

When I could speak I said, "Why him? I wish it'd been me instead."

"There's much we don't understand. Maybe your mother is right and God had a reason for taking him."

"She won't talk about Uncle around me."

Aunt Azar smoothed hair away from my face. "She misses him, though she may not show it."

I shook my head, holding back curses I didn't want her to hear.

When I could talk again I asked, "What about a funeral for Uncle?" When Grandfather died, we had a funeral and a big dinner. I remember flowers and fruit and halvah.

"We talked about it." Aunt Azar wiped tears from her eyes. "Your mother and Aunt Bita decided they didn't want to bring attention to the family—to the way he died."

Something inside me twisted. Mother wanted me to go to war when my life had barely begun. She wanted me to go, possibly give up my life, but she couldn't honor Uncle for standing up for what he believed. The heavy bag of misery I'd been carrying shifted from one shoulder to the other. My sorrow turned white hot.

When they'd all gone home that day, I brought up the idea of a funeral, but Mother shook her head.

"We will not speak of it again, Reza."

"You may think you can forget, but I won't." I spat the words. "I will remind you for as long as I live." I'd never spoken to her like this, ever.

I saw surprise flicker in her eyes, then she turned and it was gone. "I'm sure of it," she said in a voice barely audible. We didn't speak for the rest of the night.

In my room I took out Uncle's wallet and hat. I looked at the photographs, the oath to remember still ringing in my ears. That night, and for weeks afterward, I fell asleep with the feel of his belongings in my fingertips.

Later when I looked back—and I had plenty of time to look back—I was amazed I tied my shoes or got dressed those mornings. Every day, I thought I saw Uncle on the street—a trick my heart played that made me miss him even more.

✳ ✳ ✳

Ebi was sad for a few days, but soon he was back to the business of being bound for war. In early April, he grabbed me at school. "I did it. I joined up, Maggot. I leave in three days."

All that was left of my world blasted apart. "Ebi. Three days? You can't!"

"Come on, buddy. Come with me."

"Your mother must be spitting nails," I said, ignoring his begging.

"She's upset, but she knows she can't change my mind, and Dad's proud."

I sank down on the concrete step. "You can't do this. This is not real."

"How many times do I have to ask, idiot? Come with me. If you sign up now, we'll be sent together." He slapped my shin. "What do you have now? It's just you and your mom."

My hands gripped the cement, already warm from the morning sun. "And she acts like I'm not here."

"Right, and it's boring here. After we enlist, it'll be something new every day."

I didn't point out that something new could also get us killed. Instead I said, "Uncle thought the war was pointless."

"Yeah, I know, Maggot, sorry, but it still made him dead. Man, don't you want to kill the bastards who took him?"

I looked at Ebi, but I didn't answer. I knew revenge wasn't the path Uncle would have wanted. But he wasn't here. I was never going to get to England or America. Anger was easier than the ache of missing him.

The bell rang. Ebi grabbed my arm. "Just think about it. For me?"

I tried to smile. "Right, like I'm going to think about anything else today?"

That night Mother said, "I hear Ebi goes to training in a few days."

"He told me."

"His parents must be proud."

I looked up at her. "What does that mean?"

"It means just what I said."

"If you lose Father, Uncle, and me? Is it still a 'good' war?"

"Whatever happens is God's will. He chooses the purest of people to be martyrs, because they are worthy of his company."

I felt like I'd eaten a green chili whole. I took a deep breath to quiet the heat in my face and head and chest. "God's will. How do you know what God's will is?" I was at the window in three steps so she couldn't see my tears. "Did God tell you why your brother had to die?"

"Stop that, Reza." Her voice was high and shrill. She stood up and cleared my plate. I'd only taken three bites.

"It is unacceptable for you to speak that way. The voice of God will not be questioned in this house." She kept wiping her hands on her apron, though I was sure they were dry. "Your grandfather would be horrified to hear you talk like that. He always said—"

"Fine," I interrupted. I was so tired of hearing about it. "I'll join tomorrow. You can hold your head high in the mosque." I walked to my room and slammed the door, surprised by the decision I'd made. But I'd lost so many people who mattered to me. No way was I going to lose Ebi, too.

CHAPTER SEVEN

I woke before first light and dressed quickly. As I ran through the cool, empty streets, the wind whispered behind me, *Do it now, don't think anymore, do it now.* I had to wait outside the recruiter's office until it opened, but the man who unlocked the door didn't look surprised to see me there so early.

"You're here to sign up?" It was barely a question.

I didn't say "I'm here to do what my mother wants me to do, because that's what I always do" or "It's the only thing left for me to do." I just nodded and said, "Yes . . . yes, sir."

"We have a group of boys going at the end of the week."

He pointed to a table and handed me a stack of forms. A few I had to take home for Mother to fill out. The rest I did myself. I paused for morning prayers, and by the time I'd finished all the paperwork, I had ten minutes to get to school.

"You are doing a great service to God," said the recruiter in a voice that sounded like a recording. "Come back on Friday morning. We leave at nine."

I ran to make the bell and slipped into a desk beside Ebi just as class began.

He gave me a quizzical look, but I looked straight ahead. My mind was a thousand other places. Would I ever see the sun stream through the schoolroom window again? Would I see any of the other guys who'd left for the front in the last month? Would I kill someone?

I don't know how much time went by as I sat daydreaming, but Ebi kicked me and motioned to the front of the room.

"Reza, can you answer this question?" asked Mr. Tarighian.

"I . . . I . . . I'm sorry, sir, what was the question?" My face went crimson.

"Mr. Mirzai, I know this is the first class of the day, but I suggest you wake up and pay attention."

"Yes, sir." I picked up my pencil and turned my notebook to a blank sheet.

Before I'd written a word, Ebi shoved a folded note onto the page. I opened it carefully. "What's up?" was written in his careless scrawl.

When Mr. Tarighian turned to the board, I scribbled on the other side of his note. "I'm coming with you."

I passed the note to Ebi. From the corner of my eye, I watched him unfold the scrap.

As he read, he jerked toward me, sending books clattering to the floor. The noise masked Ebi's low whoop.

Mr. Tarighian turned around. "Mr. Saberi, what seems to be the problem?"

"I'm sorry sir," said Ebi. "I . . . I accidentally knocked my books off my desk."

Mr. Tarighian raised his eyebrows but said only, "See that it doesn't happen again."

"Yes, sir," he said, hiding a grin behind his hand.

After class Ebi waited until we were in the hall to grab me in a crushing bear hug.

"You happy now?" I asked.

"This is gonna be great!" Ebi danced from foot to foot as we walked to the next class. "We're going to smash 'em."

We left school in the afternoon, the exact same way we had for as long as I could remember. At the end of the block, Ebi stopped.

"Let's get a soda and hang out in the market for a while. We can watch the girls on their way home."

I started, "I can't, I've got—"

"Homework? You don't need to do your homework, stupid. Day after tomorrow, homework is a thing of the past." Ebi laughed and walked the other way toward the market.

I hesitated a split second, then was right behind him. We spent two hours sitting on a low stone wall. The blue and yellow mosaics of the mosque glittered like sapphires as the sun dipped toward the western edge of the city. We shared an orange and some chocolate and watched women shop at the huge bins of almonds, cashews, and pistachios. We each bought a soda and when we were finished, bought another.

I hadn't felt this normal since the morning Uncle had visited weeks before. I started humming. Being careful no one could hear me, I sang all the way home.

As I opened the door of the apartment, my mouth watered at the smell of onion and something else I couldn't place. I was normally home before Mother, but today we'd lost track of time. I thought she might be angry, but when I came into the kitchen, she stood there with a thin smile on her face.

"Hello, son. You and Ebi have been wasting time, I assume. I'm glad you're home. I made *Khoresht-e Fesenjan*."

I loved chicken in pomegranate sauce. Mother hadn't made it in a long time—not since my birthday two years ago.

She'd heard I'd signed up. Her anger was gone. She'd been replaced by the mother I hadn't seen in years. I didn't know whether to run or to stay for as long as it lasted.

I stood and stared.

"What?" she asked. "Why do you stand there like a stone?"

"How did you hear?"

"Ours is a small community, Reza, and news travels quickly. We will talk about it over dinner. Your aunt will be here soon."

As I washed my hands, I listened to her setting the table. I was leaving to fight a war and she was happy. I'd half hoped, when it came down to it, that she'd react like Ebi's mother and beg me to stay.

Aunt Azar opened the door and called, "Reza, Sameera, I'm here."

When we sat, Mother wasted no time on small talk. "I understand you leave on Friday morning. Do you know where they are sending you?"

"The man who signed me up said something about going south to the assault on Basra, but we won't know till we're on our way."

"Wouldn't that be nice," said Aunt Azar. Her smile looked as if it were taped on her face. "It is beautiful there."

"He is not going on holiday, Azar," said Mother. "He is going to serve his God."

"Yes, of course," said Aunt Azar. "We are all proud, Reza." She poured tea. "I know it's not my place to say." She looked at Mother and quickly looked away again. "But, Reza, are you sure you want to go?" Once she'd said it, her words poured out like ants from a smashed hill. "Everyone says they are going to make boys your age sign up soon enough, but you don't have to go yet. Maybe the struggle will be over before you have to go." She took one of my hands in hers. "So many young boys have gone and not come back. Are you afraid?"

"Afraid?" Mother's moment of kindness was gone. Her eyes shone with their old fierceness. "No son of mine is afraid. He'll fight bravely and come home a hero or die a martyr in this holy war."

"Sister," said Aunt Azar, "before the revolution, we were taught the Prophet's message was about peace, not violence."

"Our Prophet had many teachings of peace, but going to battle in self-defense is holy."

I tapped my fork on the edge of the plate. "Uncle said this stopped being about self-defense when we invaded Iraq. If this isn't a holy war and I die, maybe I won't go to heaven; maybe I'll end up in hell."

Aunt Azar gasped. Mother stood over me and said in a loud

voice, "Enough of what your uncle said. The holy men teach us to believe the power of God over all things. We, in our limited knowledge, cannot truly know what is right or wrong. The holy men bring us God's word. They would not ask for our sacrifice if it were not necessary."

It was like she had a script and she'd been reading it so long, she had no words of her own. What I wanted most in that moment was to be small enough to fit under the crook of her arm in a way I could barely remember, to have her read to me when I still fit on her lap. I ran my hand over my face.

"Mother, the Iraqis honor Muhammad just like us." I pulled the plastic key from my pocket and waved it in the air. "Are the boys in Baghdad given keys, too? Will we all get to heaven and share the mansions and the riches?"

Mother's jaw twitched, the only movement in her tight face. "Go to your room. Not another word. I pray God will forgive you."

She stared at me and I stared back. Finally, I went over to Aunt Azar, who sat openmouthed.

"Good-bye, Auntie. Thank you for coming." She hugged me tight, then wiped her eyes with the back of her hand.

I sat in my room, listening to Auntie and Mother talking in low voices. The smells of other dinners, in other homes, wafted through my open window. After a while, because I always had,

I did my homework. Then, even though it was still early, I went to bed and lay awake, staring at the dark ceiling.

If God paid attention the way Mother believed, did Uncle's death qualify him for heaven? He died fighting for a cause he believed in, but was it for the right side? If I died, maybe Uncle would be there, too, standing at the door of our own mansion. And if it really was heaven, there would be music, and we could sing and play with Mr. Monk and Mr. Parker.

CHAPTER EIGHT

Friday morning, when I woke, Mother was gone. On the table were a few rial coins and a note: *Reza, may God watch over you.*

I held the note in my hand. My eyes landed on a framed picture on the wall. Mother and I smiling on my first day of school, her hand resting on my shoulder. I crumpled the note, dropped it at my feet, and left the money untouched. I wondered if she'd look at that picture when she was all alone.

I put a few books, a toothbrush, and Uncle's hat into a bag. His wallet and the last tape went into my pants pocket.

Outside the recruiting office the street was full of families clustered around boys. The sun shone down on the mosque, sending reflected colors across the square. Kids were laughing and mothers were trying to hide tears.

Ebi's family was at the edge of the crowd. His little brothers ran circles around his red-eyed mother, raising a ring of ochre dust. Ebi waved.

"Hey, Maggot, over here."

"Hello, Reza," said Ebi's father. "Is your mother on her way?"

"No, sir, she couldn't make it this morning."

"Oh, I'm sorry." He glanced at his wife.

"We've enough family here for the both of you," said Ebi's mother, motioning to the crowd of cousins, all hugging Ebi and slapping him on the back.

For twenty minutes we listened to advice from old grandpas. We joked with the boys and avoided sad looks from the women. One of Ebi's aunts had *sangak* already spread with tomato and feta. She'd gone to market especially early for Ebi's last day. The warm bread was soft and chewy at the same time. We ate and licked our fingers clean.

A soldier came out of the office, standing in front of the door until the crowd was quiet.

"Welcome, young soldiers. Welcome, families. These boys are embarking on the most honored mission of their lives, a mission to keep us all safe."

Cheers rose from the crowd, but I heard sobbing, too. This time I held my fist high above my head like the others. I was on my way—ready to be anywhere but here.

We waited for uniforms and equipment. The line moved quickly. "Next time I see you, you'll look the part, pal," said Ebi as we were ushered to different rooms.

Eight of us milled around in a large room with benches along the walls. Every few feet was a box. On top of each box was a rifle.

"Whoa—look at these," said the boy next to me, holding his new gun. "It's a Kalashnikov. I've never seen one this close."

"Yeah, I wonder when they'll give us bullets," said another. We all laughed. For a minute, laughing loosened the fist that was squeezing my chest.

In the box was a neatly folded green uniform. Clean, but faded, not new. I didn't want to think who else had worn it and why it wasn't his anymore.

I carefully slipped Uncle's wallet and tape into my new pants pocket. I yanked on the heavy boots and became a soldier.

Outside, the sun had moved higher in the sky. Sweat trick-led down my neck under the heavy green helmet, so I took it off and worked my way over to Ebi and his family again.

Seeing my old friend in his new outfit was like looking in a mirror—we looked years older in our worn canvas jackets. Dressed in green from helmet to boot, Ebi's only splash of color was a brand-new *shemagh*. One of his uncles was adjusting the red-and-white-checked head covering and the thick black rope of fabric that held the scarf in place. Someone else strapped a rusty canteen over one of his shoulders. Ebi held his rifle, while another uncle taped a picture of Ayatollah Khomeini to the stock.

"Reza, looking sharp." Ebi grabbed my helmet and put it back on my head.

"You, too. The *shemagh* is nice."

"A gift from my aunt," Ebi said as he swept his arm around the oldest woman in the crowd and kissed her cheek noisily. The family's laughter was drowned out by the sound of two huge trucks rounding the corner.

"This is it," yelled the recruiter. "Say your good-byes and line up. These trucks are leaving in five minutes."

Immediately, Ebi was lost in a sea of family—a tumult of kisses, hugs, and tears. I stood on the outskirts of the throng. I got a few encouraging handshakes and a hug from Ebi's little sister, but then I had to step away. I watched his father and too many uncles who weren't mine. I watched until Ebi came and dragged me toward the line.

"Come on, buddy. One more minute and my mother will take me home."

We climbed into the back of the open truck. Hard metal benches lined the inside of the bed. Twelve boys to a side, we stood against metal rails, facing out to the shouting crowd. Some women held handkerchiefs, and as everyone boarded, the cheering got louder and louder. We waved our arms in the air like rock stars.

Just before we pulled away, Ebi grabbed my sleeve and pointed. There, at the end of the block, away from the crowd, Mother stood, her arms at her sides. Our eyes met; she raised her hand just to her shoulder. She may have nodded, but I turned away before I was sure. I had a thousand images of our life together, but the picture of her standing there was all I saw until we'd left the city far behind.

* * *

We traveled south for hours, stopping once for water and once for a lunch of cheese and yogurt that we ate in the truck. During lunch they collected our rifles, putting them all in a jeep that headed back the way we'd come. Someone guessed they were just part of the send-off show. The warm wind and the rumble of the truck made it too noisy for much talk, but sometimes someone would yell loud enough for the rest of us to hear.

A few hours in, Ebi caught my eye, pointed to the long horizon, and yelled, "See, I knew this would be good. We're real warriors now, my friend. Just like on TV."

I considered pointing out that if I'd been watching TV, my butt wouldn't be so sore from bouncing up and down, but instead I nodded and watched our progress through the desert. I pushed away the image of Mother alone in the dusty street.

As the sun headed to the horizon, the light cast a golden glow on our faces. I caught a whiff of sea air, even though the water was still probably an hour away. Just then, I guess Ebi realized no one could hear us in this open country. He looked around, his eyes sparkling with mischief.

"Guys, we could sing any song we want out here! I don't think even the driver can hear us."

He half stood, swinging his hips back and forth, and sang, "Well, you can tell by the way I use my walk I'm a woman's man; no time to talk." We laughed, then one by one the rest of us joined in until the chorus of the popular disco song "Stayin' Alive" reached a crescendo.

Our voices boomed in harmony with the sound of the truck as we went through all the songs that we'd not been able to sing for years, each boy yelling out his favorite. Ebi beat the rhythm with his hands on the metal bench. Sitting across from him, I drummed, too, as we saw tents materialize in the distance.

Ebi was singing in his loudest voice, almost screaming, when he stopped, like the last note had gotten stuck in his throat. The color drained from his face, and his eyes fixed on something over my shoulder. The boys on either side of him followed his gaze. On my side we all stopped singing and swung around.

There, stacked in piles of three or four, were bodies, face up or face down, the green canvas of their uniforms covered in desert sand. Green canvas uniforms just like ours. Three buzzards circled above them. Legs and arms shot out at odd angles, stiff like steel. I'd never seen a dead body before. Not even my grandparents'. I knew Ebi hadn't, either. Some were missing limbs. And there was blood. So much blood.

I started to shake, shivering like I had a fever. We saw stacks every ten meters for the next few minutes. Why were they here? Were they waiting to be buried? As we watched, a huge buzzard—this one bigger than the others—circled and landed, gazing at us as we rattled by.

No one looked away. As we passed the last pile, I noticed a man's face. He had a short black beard that looked just like my father's.

Without thinking I leaped up on the bench, ready to jump out of the truck. Ebi grabbed the waistband of my pants.

"Reza, what are you doing?"

"I . . . that looked like . . ." I didn't finish, realizing Ebi, and everyone else on the truck, would think I was crazy if I said it looked like my father, who'd been dead for over a year.

We spent the rest of the trip in silence.

CHAPTER NINE

I'd stopped shaking but still felt sick by the time we stopped. We all staggered out of the truck. A soldier, clipboard in hand, read off tent assignments. I stayed close to Ebi, crossing my fingers behind my back like a little kid, hoping we'd get the same tent. Until that moment it hadn't occurred to me we might be separated here. I wouldn't be able to stand that. I held my breath as boys in front of us peeled off in different directions. I almost kissed the man when he said number ten after both our names. He pointed down a long row of squat tents. We shouldered our bags and headed in the direction of our temporary home.

"Thanks for keeping me from jumping out of the truck." I rubbed one hand over my eyes. "For a few weird seconds, I thought I saw my dad lying there on one of those piles." I shuddered again, thinking about what we'd seen.

I wanted Ebi to say something funny—something to make me laugh. But he only shook his head and said, "I don't think it's that weird. I mean, what's normal when you see your first dead body?" He let out a long breath. "And it wasn't just a dead body, Rez. That was . . . I don't know what that was, but . . ." He didn't finish, just shook his head.

We stood together at the wide tent flap. Once this tent had been white, but the desert wind had turned it a burnt nutty color. The air was bone-dry, and in the time it had taken us to walk from the truck, it made my teeth feel like sandpaper against my tongue.

As I scanned the light brown of the distant dunes, I was hit by a memory of the turquoise and maroon bazaar stalls, the deep greens and soft pinks of the almond trees in spring. I heard the call to prayer, the way the notes sounded from my bedroom window. All the colors and sounds of home flashed in my mind and then were buried by the sandy beige at my feet.

The tent had twelve rickety canvas cots standing a few

inches off the dusty ground, each with a rough brown blanket folded at the bottom.

"Hope none of you snore," said a boy already arranging his bag at the head of the nearest cot. "'Cause if you do, you're sleeping out in the sand."

It was something Ebi would have said. I looked to see if he was laughing, but his shoulders were slumped and his eyes had a vacant look I'd never seen before. We lay down on bunks next to each other without talking. I wanted to close my eyes, but when I did, all I saw were bodies stacked up like lumber.

An hour later we were called to a huge open-sided canopy for supper. Ebi and I shuffled past the rough wooden tables and benches, choosing a spot at the far end.

"This tastes like dirt," said Ebi, spitting out his first bite.

"It's just the sand that's already stuck between your teeth," I said. I looked around. You could tell who'd just come in today by their clean shirts and the faces they made as they tasted the food.

A stocky soldier, probably fifteen or sixteen, sat down. With a crooked smile he reached over me and took a potato off Ebi's plate.

"First day here?" We nodded. He raised his voice to be heard over a group of guys streaming in and grabbing plates from a central table. "You get used to the gravelly desert taste. When

I go home, I'm asking my mom to add sand to all my favorite dishes."

He'd obviously used the line before, but I didn't mind. It brought a smile to Ebi's face.

"I'm Kamran." He grabbed my hand, pumping it like he was filling a water bucket. He took Ebi's and did the same. His short dark hair stood straight up in places. I wondered if he'd cut it himself without a mirror. "Where are you guys from?"

"Shiraz," I answered for both of us. "You?"

"Outside of Tehran, near the mountains."

Ebi looked up from his untouched plate. "How long have you been here?"

Kamran scratched his chin. "I've been based at this camp for two months—longer than most."

"Where do guys go from here?" Ebi asked.

Kamran hesitated for a second. "You'll hear about that later." He looked at our plates. "You better eat up. It all tastes this bad. Get used to it."

We picked at our food while Kamran talked. He told a funny story about a general who sang in his sleep, and he talked about Tehran. A guy walked by and rubbed Kamran's head, saying, "I'm shipping out tomorrow, Kam."

Kamran smiled. "Good luck."

"What'll we do here all day?" I asked.

"You'll work hard at doing nothing." Kamran laughed at his own joke. "Sometimes they pretend to train you to use those huge rifles they carry, but mostly we get good at sitting and waiting."

A kid sauntered up to the table. He looked younger than us, but I didn't ask. As I looked around, I realized nobody looked older than twenty. The kid nodded at us and then, as the last guy had, he rubbed Kamran's head, saying, "Kamran, bring me home."

I raised my eyebrows and shot Ebi a quizzical look. "What's going on?"

Kamran's cheeks reddened. "Some guys are superstitious, is all." He stood up and brushed a nonexistent crumb from his pant leg. "I better get back to my tent. Good to meet you guys."

I caught his sleeve. "What do you mean, superstitious?"

Kamran shifted from one foot to the other. "Well—it's kinda wild, but I guess I've been to the front and back more than any other guy in camp. Someone came up with the idea that if they rubbed my head, it'd bring them luck."

"How many times have you gone?" I asked.

"Four," said Kamran, his eyes on his feet. When he raised his eyes, he looked straight at us and lowered his voice. "We aren't supposed to talk about it, but I won't lie to you guys. It's hell. Lots of guys die there, or are captured and sent to prisoner-of-war camps in Iraq."

"Kamran," a boy yelled from several tables over, "bring that lucky head over here."

He gave us a small wave and said, "Anyway, welcome aboard. See you around."

✳ ✳ ✳

Later the camp was quiet, but I couldn't sleep. I sat outside the tent and watched the stars. Since Dad died, then Uncle, sometimes it felt like death was *all* I thought of, but I'd never really thought it could happen to me—or to Ebi.

The tent flap rustled and Ebi sat down, his new red-and-white scarf hanging around his neck.

"It cools down, huh?" he asked, but I didn't think he really wanted an answer.

So I said, "I can barely find the constellations with all these stars—so different from home."

A huge shooting star sped across the sky. We both watched but didn't say anything.

"Rez, what have I gotten us into? All those bodies."

"I know. It was . . ." I didn't know what it was so I let the sentence sit between us.

"*You* knew it wasn't going to be like the movies, didn't you?" Ebi said quietly.

"I guess."

"Remember when we used to play soldiers in the park?"

"Sure."

"Remember that huge tree?"

"How we were so scared of climbing it?" I finished his thought.

"Exactly." Ebi scrubbed his face with his hand. "But this is the real thing, isn't it?"

I let my breath out slowly. "You mean something real to be scared of?"

"Exactly." He picked up a handful of sand and let it drain through his fingers. "If you knew, why did you come?"

"To be somewhere other than home," I answered, scooping up a handful of sand myself. "To be with you."

"But what if we both get killed?"

The question hung in the dry air, feeding the fear we were learning to name. Maybe it was better to have it spoken. We could joke about it now. I said, "Well, then we'll go to heaven and have all the girls and money and anything else we want—right?" I lightly punched his arm.

Ebi looked up at the sparkling sky. "Maybe I should've asked before we got here, but do you believe in all that? Do you believe God is watching us right now?"

A desert owl *hoot-hoot*ed in the distance. I said, "When I

asked Uncle about heaven he said some people call it 'a home that will last.' That seems more believable to me than the huge mansions and stuff. I know I should believe it. Mother sure does. I guess you don't get proof until you're dead."

I pulled my jacket closer, and one of my favorite tunes floated through my head. "What I don't get is how God can make music and pomegranates and killing, too."

I felt Ebi nod beside me. "I wish there was a holy man I could ask, but I'd be afraid to."

The canvas behind us flapped in the gentle breeze.

"We'd better get some sleep," I said. As we turned toward the tent, I smelled the desert finally giving up some of its heat for the morning dew.

CHAPTER TEN

A clanging bell woke us early the next morning. Breakfast was bread, butter, sand, and jam. Soon after we sat down, a young officer rapped us on the backs of our heads.

"Outside in ten minutes. Line up behind tent four."

Dozens of us shuffled into line. The breeze of the night before was gone, like a ghost you swear you saw but doubted at first light. We were there for a rally, a repeat of the one we'd heard at school, but these soldiers looked hollow and worn around the edges, as if their words had been recorded years ago and now the tape was stretched and brittle.

As they talked about the glorious struggle, we cheered and waved our fists in the air, but we glanced sideways at each other and quickly looked away.

Then as Kamran had warned, for weeks we sat in one place or another—mostly waiting. Every few days we were told stories of Hussain ibn Ali, the Prophet's grandson, who stood alone against an army of thousands. We joined in the call to prayer. We got used to the gritty food. We listened to gunfire far off in the distance.

The World Cup would start in about two months. What with the revolution and the war, Iran had pulled out, but we still talked about who was going to be in it. Every time a truck came in with new recruits, we grilled them for scores. Once we were even allowed to listen to part of a game on the radio. But most days we traded stories with boys from other towns, and when no one was looking we played cards for coins we didn't have.

New recruits came in every day, and almost as often thirty to forty guys loaded into trucks and went to the front. Kamran was right; most of them didn't come back, and those who did didn't talk about it. One day as we watched a dozen boys limp back into camp, Ebi asked something I'd been wondering. "How come so many die? Are the Iraqis that much better than us? Do our guns suck?"

"They're probably not all dead. Remember, Kamran said some end up in POW camps."

"That sounds worse than dying," said Ebi. "Especially if you believe the stuff about the mansions and the girls."

One morning an older soldier took us to the far end of camp for shooting practice. The Kalashnikov rifle felt like a cannon by the time we had walked the full length of the camp with the guns on our shoulders.

The first time I pulled the trigger, the butt of the big gun slammed back so hard, I staggered. After half a dozen tries, I stood without falling, but the bullet rarely hit the target. Ebi was no better.

"And I thought this would be fun," he said as we made our way back to our tent after the practice.

"Remember the time Uncle Habib took us to the country to shoot BB guns?"

"I remember, Maggot. Now, that was fun." He shifted his gun from one shoulder to the other and groaned. "Those little guns and these honkers are not made on the same planet."

"Right," I said, looking for a comfortable hold on my own gun. "I feel like I could practice for months but I wouldn't be any better until I grew six inches. These are just too big."

A few days went by, but we didn't use the big rifles again. Ebi asked, "You think we stunk so bad they decided we were hopeless?"

"Maybe they'll train us with smaller guns," I said. But there was no more training until the day of the European Cup final. They made ten of us go to machine gun training, even though most of the camp got to gather around a radio in the mess hall.

"I can't believe we have to miss this game," Ebi said as he kicked up dust. "They may not let us listen to another."

"I bet Kamran that Peter Withe would score at least one goal."

The captain came up behind us. "All right, men. Enough talking. Lie flat on your stomachs behind a gun, upper bodies resting on your forearms." We lay down. The ground underneath us was cracked and scaled like lizard skin.

"That's right," said the captain. "Now support the barrel on the short metal legs and hold the other end near your face."

The gun was easier to shoot than the rifle, but with every *rat-a-tat-tat*, my eyes and nose filled with yellow dirt. I held my breath so my mouth wouldn't fill up, too. As we trudged back to camp afterward, I swore to myself that if I ever got to see actors using machine guns in a movie again, I'd figure out how they made it look so easy.

"I wonder which gun we'll carry to the front," said Ebi.

"All I want right now is to get this crud out of my eyes. I need another shower."

At home I took a shower whenever I wanted, but here we only got one shower a week on a preassigned day. The trip to the shooting range had left us hot and caked with grit. Our shower had been the day before, and the thirty seconds we got at the communal sink today wasn't going to do the job. After we washed, we moved a little way off to sit under a lean-to. From there we could see the heads of the lucky boys showering.

"This is torture to watch," said Ebi. Each shower was in a small wooden enclosure. On the outside of the door, grungy uniforms hung on a row of hooks.

"I was hoping some spray would come our way if we sat close enough," I said.

Kamran appeared and sat next to us. "Excellent, just the men I've been looking for."

I raised my eyebrows.

"I've got a job for you—something I've been thinking of doing for days, but I need help. Are you guys up for a little prank?"

"What kind of prank?" I asked.

"When the next group of lucky fools comes in to wash, we run along the outside of the stalls and grab their clothes.

We dump them at the door of the mess tent and speed back here in time to see the reaction."

There was a glint in Ebi's eyes I hadn't seen for weeks.

"What if we get caught?" I asked, looking around for an authority figure.

"I'm not worried," said Kamran. "What are they going to do, send us home?"

"Point," said Ebi, smiling.

"Okay then, get up and be ready on my mark." He gestured to the end of the stalls. "Make sure you grab the towels, too."

After the next set of boys trooped into the showers, Kamran whispered, "Wait until they're soapy."

I still wasn't sure this was a good idea, but Ebi pulled me up, saying, "Come on, man. We could use some fun."

A minute later Kamran whispered, "Okay, follow my lead."

Before I knew it, my arms held four of the stiff canvas uniforms and towels. I followed Ebi and Kamran, flying around the tents. I couldn't believe I was doing this. As we came up to the mess tent, I heard someone yell, "Hey, you boys, what's the meaning of this?"

Panic and the rush of adrenaline shared space in my throat.

Kamran yelled, "Drop them here and keep running! Heads down and follow me." He ran fast for someone so short, and

I sprinted to keep up with him. Within seconds the three of us landed in a heap under the lean-to, panting and laughing.

The boy in the first shower reached over the enclosure, eyes closed, for his towel. His hand flailed in the air. A second later all the boys realized their clothes and towels were gone.

"What the . . ."

"Hey, who took my stuff?"

Shouts and accusations filled the air.

A crowd gathered. The three of us laughed harder than we had in months. Boys streamed out of the showers all at once, some trying to hide themselves as they ran, others not bothering. Someone yelled, "Mess tent, suckers," and the clump of naked bodies headed in that direction.

By dinner everyone knew who'd pulled off the trick. We sat with Kamran, enjoying a meal complete with jabs and winks and the rubbing of Kamran's head.

✻ ✻ ✻

A few days later, Kamran found us in the shade of our tent in the late afternoon. His eyes were on the horizon over our shoulders.

"Well, boys, I guess I'll rub my own head." He ruffled his haphazard hair. We both swiveled to look at him. "They're shipping me out again tomorrow morning."

"You'd better come back, man," I said. "This camp would be totally boring without you here."

Ebi skipped a rock across the sand. "I heard them talking at lunch. They're moving a lot of people next week."

"Guess that means we might go, too." I looked off into the wavering heat.

"Hey, Kamran," Ebi said, throwing another rock. "Maybe we should rub your head, in case we get orders while you're gone."

"I'm not saying good-bye. I'll see you in a few days and we'll think of a new prank to pull," Kamran said. I ran my palm across his spiky head. Ebi did the same. Kamran leaned back, stretching at the waist from side to side. "And if I don't make it back here, assume I just got sent somewhere else. Come look me up when you get to Tehran." He bowed and turned away.

We watched until he disappeared behind a tent at the other end of camp.

"I almost wish we could go with him," said Ebi. "I'm going crazy doing nothing here, and somehow I think Kam could even make dying fun."

Two days later we were walking toward the mess tent when a covered truck full of soldiers pulled up. I recognized some of the guys who had shipped out with Kamran.

Like a line of ants, guys in grimy uniforms slowly marched toward the tents. There were bandages and wrapped wrists and ankles. None of them looked at one another or at any of us. When the last boy filed off and it wasn't Kamran, Ebi raced to the truck and peered in to make sure.

I grabbed the arm of an older boy near the end of the line. "Do you know Kamran?"

The boy gave me a dull look. "Everyone knows Kamran."

"He's not here?" Ebi said in a stunned tone.

"No," said the boy.

"Is he . . . ?" I couldn't finish the question.

"No one knows," said the boy. "We didn't find him, but he didn't come back with us, either."

"Thanks," I whispered. The boy nodded and walked away.

We went to dinner but couldn't eat. Finally I said, "It doesn't mean he's gone, Ebi. He said we'd find him in Tehran after this is over."

"I guess." The sadness in his voice was peppered with something else. It sounded like the same thing I felt, the thing that made me want to put my head on the table and cover it with my arms and stay that way for a long time.

As we sat silently, an officer came into the tent and paced from table to table, handing out slips of paper. Ebi and I looked at each other. Without a word, we knew.

"Our orders," I said.

"Maybe we'll be back for the first games of the Cup," Ebi said as he pushed his plate aside.

"What if we walked out?" I said. "We could find some small town, some family to take us in. You think they'd miss us here?"

Ebi laughed, but I was half-serious.

Every few tables the officer stopped and leaned over, delivered the paper, and said a few words. I remembered something I'd read in a book—"His blood ran cold." By the time the officer came to our table, I knew what those words meant. I squeezed Ebi's hand on the bench between us. The man said our names and told us what time to report. We'd only been in this training camp for a few weeks. Nothing about me was trained for what we might face at the front.

CHAPTER ELEVEN

Lucky you," said one of our tent mates. "You get a second shower this week."

"I guess they want you to be clean when you face the enemy," said another.

"Ebi, give me back that deck of cards before you get out of here," said a third.

It took us no time to pack. By lunch we were gone. Before sunset we laid out blankets in another camp.

This place wasn't much more than an overnight camping

spot, an oasis with a few palm trees in the middle of dunes and more dunes as far as we could see. Dinner was cold, served straight from cans, and the only choice of drink was warm, sandy water. A group gathered around and talked, but Ebi and I headed for our blankets. This camp had no tents, only tarps pulled over open trenches. I tried not to think of a grave as I lay down. I closed my eyes and pictured Aunt Azar's garden with its troughs of rich dirt where I helped plant vegetables every spring. Who would help her this year?

"Weird." Ebi finally spoke. "The truck with all the guns didn't come with us."

"Maybe it's coming in the morning."

We heard shots in the distance—much clearer here than at the old camp. There were several minutes of a volley back and forth.

"Hear that?" Ebi pushed himself up on his elbows.

"Hear what? All I hear are the birds singing in the almond groves of Shiraz."

"Oh. Yeah. Now I hear that, too." Ebi gave a hollow laugh and lowered himself.

A few minutes passed, then Ebi said, "If we get sent to different places, or if we get captured, we'll find each other, right?"

Reaching over in the dark, I rubbed his head. "It's a promise, idiot."

"Even if it's not until we get home. We'll go to the market, watch girls . . ." Ebi's voice trailed off.

"Count on it."

We lay without talking for a long time, and in the morning I wasn't sure I'd fallen asleep.

I watched the sun come up behind peach-colored cottonball clouds on the horizon. Breakfast tasted worse than dinner. Everyone shuffled around without conversation.

After a second cup of tea, I sat back down beside Ebi. "Next time we're getting ready for a football match and I act nervous, will you remind me about this morning?"

He snorted. "We thought those games were life and death."

"Next time we'll know better."

We were loaded onto a truck with oversized tires made to handle the desert and drove down a narrow track for less than fifteen minutes. Piling out, we were on top of a dune, surrounded by hot sand. An encampment lay in the distance, and I thought I saw a town just beyond that, but the horizon shimmered in the heat, blurring my vision.

"Is that what we're trying to take?" asked a small boy, pointing to the encampment.

"It is," replied the soldier who'd driven us. "It's not as far as it looks. We'll charge them together. When we take that camp, we'll bring more troops in and attack the town in a few days."

As he spoke two other trucks arrived. Within minutes sixty of us stood looking at one another. We were all teenagers. Wouldn't our odds be better if there were some soldiers with experience here? I tried to push away the panic creeping up from the soles of my feet.

"We need you in three rows—twenty across. We'll carry your weapons until we get a little closer," said a soldier.

A driver unloaded rifles, but when he finished, no more than a dozen leaned against the truck. Ebi stood in the row in front of me.

Beginning on one side, the officers took a sturdy rope and tied it around each boy's waist, attaching him to the boy next to him. We all looked around, confused.

"This is so we don't get lost or separated, especially if there's a dust storm," said the officer in charge.

Ebi turned back and said, "A dust storm? It feels like the wind hasn't come near here in years."

"I guess dust storms can come fast," I said, looking at the blue sky.

"On my command," the officer went on, "you'll run down this dune and straight ahead. Don't sprint; keep a steady pace."

I tried to smile at Ebi to hide the cold sweat I felt gathering at the base of my neck. I flashed him a wave, and he gave me one, too, but it wasn't the fist in the air from a few weeks ago.

Suddenly the man behind us roared, "May God grant victory to our army. May God defeat our enemy and its allies. May God make their children orphans and their women widows. God is good; we sacrifice for God. Hold up your keys, boys!" Many boys reached for the golden plastic keys around their necks. I left mine under my shirt.

"If you die today, you are all bridegrooms," the officer continued, his voice trembling now. "Think of this as your wedding day. God is waiting to welcome you to his kingdom."

I looked around to see the man's face. I tried to think of something funny to say to Ebi, but the line began to move. I watched my feet and the ground in front of me. If one of us fell, we'd all fall together.

I hurried to keep up. Wait. Why were the officers in the rear of the group? Shouldn't they lead the way—dust storm or not? Fear smoldered like coal in the pit of my stomach.

The distance between the lines grew. Ebi was still in front of me, but he was twenty meters away. We'd only been jogging along for a few minutes when it happened. I heard it before I felt it—a deep booming noise. Then high-pitched screams.

A huge fireball exploded near the front of the line, where the first boys were running.

It reminded me of the cloud I'd seen during breakfast, but

it wasn't fluffy or peachy. It was deep orange like hot lava—its billowed edges were jet black.

"Keep moving, boys," snarled a voice from behind.

Keep moving? Was he serious? My eardrums throbbed with a scream. In a second that lasted an hour, I realized it was mine.

In that same second, adrenaline sped through my body like a match lighting dry straw.

Then I understood. We would never get rifles. We weren't tied together to keep from getting lost. We were tied together so that when the truth hit—hit like a kick in the solar plexus—we couldn't run away. Ebi and I—and all these other boys—we weren't soldiers. We were legs and arms they didn't mind losing. We were here to die. We were human rags, walking straight into a minefield to wipe it clean.

I tried to turn, to stop where I was and yell, but I was dragged into hell by the boys who hadn't figured it out.

Another mine exploded in front of Ebi's line. He looked back at me, and I saw the exact moment of recognition on my best friend's face.

It was the last thing I saw.

My feet left the ground and I flew through the air.

A searing pain shot through my lungs. Then I felt nothing at all.

CHAPTER TWELVE

I opened my eyes. It was black, inky black. Where was I? It was as dark as the fort Ebi and I once made from his mother's chador.

But that was a long time ago.

And where was Ebi?

My eyes adjusted, and I saw dark shapes that couldn't be in Ebi's living room. Rows of beds in a long, narrow room. Antiseptic everywhere. I was flooded by a memory of black smoke and flying bodies.

Where was Ebi?

I pulled my elbows up under me, trying to sit. Pain jolted every cell in my body. My right arm immediately buckled. I fell back onto the bed, unconscious.

When I opened my eyes again, it was later—hours or days, I didn't know. Sunlight filled the room. Someone lay to my right, head bandaged except for slits for mouth and eyes. On my left, a boy lay still, an IV line hooked up to his arm.

I clutched at my sheets. I knew I had to run from this place, but my arms and legs weren't getting the message. There had been the explosion and nothing after that. I strained to catch my breath but almost choked on the smell of boy sweat mixed with the Mercurochrome that the school nurse used for skinned knees. Arabic words floated through the room. I tried to remember the vocabulary I had learned in school.

Where was Ebi?

Every time I closed my eyes, smoke and fire reappeared behind my lids. If I didn't know what had happened to me, how could I find Ebi?

Finally panic reached my legs and I kicked at the heavy material that held me down. I struggled to sit up. A dark-skinned man in a white tunic rushed over and placed one hand on my knee and another on my shoulder. "Hold on there, Mr. Reza. Calm down. Nowhere to go today, my boy." His accent was so heavy, it took a second for me to realize he was speaking Farsi, my own language.

"Ebi . . ." My throat was bone-dry and my voice sounded gravelly, like it had never been used. "I need to find my friend."

"You need to move slowly now."

"No," I croaked. "You don't understand. I need to find . . ." I tried again to push up from the mattress, but pain came from so many places, I slumped back onto the bed.

The man leaned close. The kindness in his eyes calmed me down, but the pity made me want to run again. He put his hands on either side of my face. His big thumbs felt cool on my flushed cheeks.

"I know this is frightening, son, but listen closely. You have severe lacerations all along your torso—twenty stitches—and your right arm is broken. You were lucky."

"Lucky?" I wondered if his Farsi was that bad. Did he know what *lucky* meant?

"You didn't die or lose a limb." His hands left my face and started changing the dressing on my left shoulder. "Many boys do."

I noticed a cast on my right arm. How had I not seen this before? His words sank into my brain—*die or lose a limb.* "My friend?"

The man turned away, looking for something on the table next to the bed. "Was he with you when you went into the minefield?"

"Yes," I whispered.

He was silent as he finished with my bandages. Finally he said, "You boys came in four days ago. I can check the list. What's his name?"

"Ebi Saberi, sir."

"Drink some of this broth." He handed me a warm mug and helped me sit up. "I'll check for your friend and be back soon."

The first sip of hot liquid stung. The second was a warm summer rain that made me feel sleepy. I closed my eyes and tried to replace the fireball with football or a beach scene. Footsteps stopped at my bed. I opened an eye.

"I'm afraid he wasn't with your group," said the man.

"What does that mean?"

He hesitated. "If he survived—and I hate to tell you that it's only an *if*—he could have been sent to another hospital, or to another camp."

I winced as he applied ointment to cuts I hadn't known were on my face. I wondered what he meant by *camp*.

"I need to find him. Can I go to these other camps?"

The man rested his hand on my wrist. "Son, this is a hospital that serves several prisoner-of-war camps. Once you're well enough, you'll be placed in a camp and you could be there for a very long time. You are a prisoner of Iraq."

Prisoner? The word echoed in my mind and bounced off what he'd said about Ebi—*if he survived.*

I handed him the unfinished broth and lay back in the bed. A memory flooded my head. When I was five or six, before the revolution, they took down an old building to make way for a new shopping center downtown. We all went to watch. The streets were full of people. We might have taken a picnic. Everyone cheered when the eight-story building fell in on itself. People clapped and talked as the dust settled, and we headed home. But I kept looking over my shoulder. I knew the building had been there; then everything had turned to rubble. It was as if it never existed.

Dad, Uncle Habib, the old piano, Ebi—there was no evidence of my old life here. Not even the rubble. Tears spilled from my closed eyes and filled my ears, but I didn't care.

* * *

The man in the white shirt was replaced by another, and another. I spent hours trying to think of something other than the last time I'd seen Ebi's face.

After that first day I wasn't afraid. I mostly felt empty—cracked and dry like Maharlu Lake in a drought. I spent hours trying not to think. One day I realized I had no idea how long I'd been in the hospital. I slept. I woke, tried not to think, and slept some more. The cuts on my shoulder became scars, but the wounds in my mind wouldn't form a scab.

There was no music in the hospital and no music in my head during the day. But in my dreams I heard shrill saxophones and booming drums and no melody at all.

At some point during the first few days I was fully conscious, I noticed I was dressed in the same drab hospital scrubs as everyone else and that my jacket was missing. If it was gone, I'd lost my last tape and Uncle Habib's wallet. I'd been living at the bottom of a dark hole, but realizing my last thread with Uncle was gone made me feel like I was buried alive.

I clutched the plastic key, still on the cord around my neck. It hadn't been lost with the rest of my things, but what good had it done me? I yanked it over my head and dropped it in the trash can next to my bed. Burying my face in my pillow, I sobbed silently until sleep came again.

I no longer prayed. At first I had no idea time was passing. Once I could tell one day from the next, I couldn't physically kneel down. But as weeks went by, it wasn't the physical pain that kept me from facing Mecca with the others. It was the knot that lodged just below my heart.

How could I pray to a God that sent boys, hundreds of boys, to die? Or maybe worse, to let someone like the boy in the bed next to me sit for days on end staring into space. What kind of God could make a world full of music and fruit and girls and then take it all away? What kind of God killed all the people I loved? Every time I thought about joining the others in prayer, the knot tightened and grew.

Each day was the same as the one before. Some boys read or played cards, but not me. Unless the orderlies were talking directly to us, they spoke Arabic. Words I barely understood swirled in my head. The hours were divided by the coming and going of meal trays, the days by the coming and going of broken boys.

A few days after my cast was removed, someone across the aisle groaned, "It must be Wednesday; they're serving that tasteless crud again. Every Wednesday it's the same damn thing."

"Maybe if you eat, you'll get out of here," said the orderly who brought the tray.

"Yeah, yeah," said the boy. "But I'm right, aren't I? It's Wednesday, isn't it?"

"No, it's Thursday. Thursday, June seventeenth. Ramadan comes soon. When Ramadan starts and you have to fast all day, you'll be wishing you ate this hot meal."

Thursday, June seventeenth? My birthday. I wondered what Mother was thinking today. Did she know I was alive? If she thought I was dead, was she proud? Where would I be next year at this time? I was thirteen. I was finally thirteen, but I felt older than anyone I'd ever known.

CHAPTER THIRTEEN

Seven weeks after I was carried unconscious into the hospital, I was given a pair of bright yellow pants and a matching jacket and was ushered out the door. Feeling the sun on my face for the first time since the explosion, I squinted and hunched my shoulders against the light.

A doctor loaded me into the passenger seat of an old jeep. He helped another boy into the backseat and said, "Take care of yourselves, boys. You'll be playing football soon." He waved as the driver pulled away. "It's a short ride to the camps."

We were tossed up and down as we drove along a rutted road. There were no street signs or landmarks to tell me where I was. Somewhere in Iraq—maybe that's all I needed to know.

To the right lay a small town, just a scattering of two-story buildings. The jeep turned left and passed an old factory with high windows, shattered and filthy. In a dusty open lot, a pack of wild dogs leered as the jeep passed. Soon we came to a battered chain-link fence and a guarded gate.

The guard nodded to the jeep's driver and, waving him in, raised a large wooden barricade. Once inside, there were six more gates, three on either side, each leading to short brick buildings. Each complex was surrounded by a low concrete wall topped with barbed wire.

At the last gate stood a five-foot-high picture of a grinning Saddam Hussein. I could barely see the leader's uniform under all the ribbons and medals. I knew I was supposed to hate him, but I didn't really care. We passed the portrait, and another wooden barrier rose and dropped shut behind us. Twenty yards beyond the gate, the jeep pulled up to a small office.

"Stay here," said the driver. He grabbed a stack of papers and went inside.

"Where does he think we're going?" asked the other boy with a laugh. We'd exchanged a few two-word sentences in the hospital, but I didn't remember his name. He had a round, open face. When he smiled, it showed a gap between his two front teeth. "Superman couldn't make it over these walls with those guards standing every hundred meters. They'd fill us with holes in a millisecond."

A shudder rippled down my spine as I saw one of the soldiers toss a Kalashnikov to another. I remembered the guns they'd piled up next to the truck before they sent us into the exploding desert—the guns they never meant for us to use. I could go the rest of forever without seeing another gun like that.

Dozens of boys were hanging around the yard, some younger than me, others needing a shave. A hot, strong wind rustled their identical yellow jackets and pants. At one end of the space was a football goal marked by two boards shoved in the ground. At the other end, ruts in the dust formed the other side's net. The boys passed an old ball back and forth. I looked at them, wondering if there were any from Shiraz, or even from my school.

The driver came back and jumped behind the wheel. "Out, you two." He gestured to a boy who'd followed him from the office. "This is Salar. He'll show you around."

After we stepped into the yard, the jeep reversed, sending up billows of dust as it shot back through the open gate.

"Welcome, gentlemen," said Salar as we shook hands. He was tall and thin, all arms and legs. He swept his arm out as if presenting a palace. "It's bad, but it's not exactly jail. We get outside every day and the food isn't half sand."

"That's a welcome change," laughed my jeep companion. For the first time in months, I laughed too, and a tiny breeze of relief rippled through me.

"So you heard the man, my name's Salar. I'm from Tabriz, up north. I'm sixteen. Been here a year and a half." He pointed to me. "And you?"

"A year and a half?" I croaked.

"Like I said, it's no fun." Salar shrugged. "But since we might all be here awhile, what's your name?"

"Reza. I'm from Shiraz." The sound of my voice in the open air seemed strange. Salar nodded and turned to the other boy.

"I'm Jaafer." He pointed to himself. "From outside Birjand."

"I have a cousin in Birjand. Used to visit every—" Salar was interrupted by a loud bell. "Aha, fine fellows, that bell means lunch." He turned abruptly to us. "Unless of course you're fasting. If you are, you could go to lockdown early or come watch us eat. Either of you fasting?"

We both shook our heads, mumbling no. Ramadan had begun and I'd barely thought about it. I wondered if my aunts and uncles were coming to feast with Mother at the end of the day. Did they talk about me?

Salar ushered us into one of the concrete buildings and down a corridor to a large hall full of boys. The windows along one side hadn't been cleaned in years. As we sat down at a table, the scent of garlic and cumin was so strong it made me squint. A boy with an apron brought an aluminum pan heaped with white rice, topped with boiled cabbage in a brown sauce. It looked like last week's leftovers, but my mouth watered all the same.

"Eat up, gentlemen," said Salar, snapping his fingers and motioning toward the food. "It tastes better than it looks."

Three boys were sitting there. Salar eased in at the head of the table and said, "Welcome our new recruits, boys. Introduce yourselves."

When the youngest, a boy named Farhad, said in a small voice, "I'm almost thirteen." I heard my own voice, a million years ago, saying the same words to Uncle Habib.

"I've only been here a few weeks," said Farhad, his voice barely audible above the din of talking boys. "I was in the hospital for five months." I followed the boy's gaze to his lap and noticed a small set of crutches. One of his legs had been amputated below the knee. I felt like I should look away, but I couldn't.

"I've been here the longest," said Omid, a boy with loose black curls that fell below his ears. He had the beginnings of a beard and a hooked nose. His mouth looked like it was on the edge of a smile, and his voice was as loud as Farhad's was quiet.

"I signed up when fighting started and landed here three weeks later. Stupid or what?"

The third boy stared at his empty plate. All I saw was jet-black hair and a razor-sharp jaw.

Salar said, "Pasha, speak up, man. Introduce yourself to the new meat." The boy scowled, then turned back to the empty plate.

"Pasha hates us, yet for some reason he continues to grace us with his presence." Salar raised his hands in the air. "It's one of the wonders of the world."

"You're so skinny, Salar." Omid let out a hearty laugh. "You're easy to abuse. Me—he just can't stay away from my good looks."

Pasha pushed the plate to the middle of the table. Standing up, he said, "It's bad enough only the youngest of you observes the holy days." I noticed then that Farhad wasn't eating either. He watched with a serene smile as Pasha said, "You sit here and do nothing but joke," and left to sit at an empty table nearby. Even his back looked angry.

Everyone glanced sheepishly at one another until Jaafer said, "Nice guy." He put another spoonful of rice on his plate. "Tell you what, if God gets me out of this hole, I'll fast every day, all month long. Until then I'm having another helping."

The rest of us laughed quietly. I took a bite and cleared my throat. "Do you guys know everyone in these camps?"

"Well, there are at least four hundred of us in these fine accommodations, and people come and go," said Salar.

"Oh, come on, Salar, you're the ambassador of this dust heap. You know everybody," teased Omid.

"I'm looking for a friend who was with me at the front." My voice shook. "His name is Ebi Saberi. He'd have come in sometime in the last month." I listed Ebi's features, realizing I was describing half the boys in the room.

"Don't know him. Sorry, man."

"You see guys from other camps?" I asked hopefully.

"Transfers come and go," said Omid.

"Maybe Miles would know," whispered Farhad.

"Who's Miles?" I asked.

"A teacher," said Salar, chewing. "Comes from a foreign aid organization. Our 'kind' captors think it looks better to the outside world if they bring in someone to educate us. Miles is the third one we've had and the best of the lot. You'll meet him tomorrow."

"Why would he know?"

"He is the main teacher here at Camp Six, but he teaches at the other camps, too."

A loud bell rang. "Time for lockup," said Salar, motioning to the door where a huge guard stood. "Come on. Mr. Abass here will show us to our deluxe suite."

The guard was dressed in faded green canvas. He stood well over six feet, his arms crossed over his chest. Under an old cap I saw one dark, bushy eyebrow stretching across his forehead. Long lines on either side of his wide nose anchored the edges of a deep frown.

The huge man led a big group of us along narrow, dark corridors that stank of boys and no soap. Our jovial lunch chatter shifted to silence as we all filed behind Farhad's crutches. Just when it seemed to me that we were traveling in circles, Abass brought out a key and opened the door to a large room.

"Move it, vermin, we don't have all day." Abass shoved Farhad into the room. The small boy fell, and his crutches spun across the floor. Jaafer and I both moved to help him up, but before we got to him Abass had a hand on our collars, pulling us upright. His breath was so rank I had to breathe through my mouth. His accent was so thick he was on to the second sentence before I understood the first.

"Time to learn, boys. Everyone here does for himself. Farhad can get up. If he ever goes home, he'll need to get along without you two."

Salar stepped in to break the tension. "Leave your shoes inside the door, gentlemen. It's not the Tehran Hilton, but it's better than a trench in the sand or that stinking hospital. Isn't that so, Mr. Abass?" Salar looked up at the guard, who gave a low grunt and walked out the door. The dead bolt echoed behind him.

"Salar," said Omid, "one of these days you'll wake that beast."

"He's a jerk," hissed Salar.

"True, but he beat those guys in Building Two for less crap than you give him, and they're still in the hospital."

"Whatever." Salar waved his fingers at the door in a rude gesture. "He smells exactly like the butt of a four-day-old fish."

Laughter filled the concrete room. Omid guffawed. "Fish Butt. That's good, Salar."

I hadn't had a belly laugh like this in so long, my muscles actually hurt, but my breath came a little easier when I was done.

The windows along the tops of the walls were dirtier than the ones in the cafeteria and too high to reach. Brown light filtered through, highlighting the dust in the air. Twenty mats lay on the floor in two long lines.

"Reza, Jaafer, those two mats at the end are yours," said Omid. "Get comfortable; we spend most of the afternoon locked up here. And despite how Salar is with old Fish Butt, you boys watch yourselves. This is one of the best camps to be in because they show it off to the newspapers and such, but if the guards think they can get away with it, they'll hurt you." He walked toward his mat and added over his shoulder, "Especially Fish Butt."

I followed Jaafer to the back of the room, but the sound of gunfire made me jump, pressing my back against the wall. Jaafer and Farhad cringed, too, but the other boys acted like they hadn't heard anything.

"Don't worry about it," said Salar when he noticed. "It's the change of shift up on the wall. They have to play with their arsenal." He cupped his crotch and laughed.

"Shut up," said Pasha, kicking Salar's mat. "At least they're still doing a job, unlike us, rotting away in this dungeon."

"Some job," said Salar. "They're guarding teenagers, while their friends are off fighting in the real war. No wonder they need to shoot their guns every day."

"We were just stupid enough to get caught." Pasha moved closer to Salar, who was at least six inches shorter.

"Back off, Pasha," said Omid, stepping in front of him. The boys stood eye to eye for twenty seconds; neither of them flinched.

Pasha was the first to back down. I heard the call to prayer from somewhere far away. Reaching under his rubber mat, Pasha spread out a large piece of fabric in the center of the room. He knelt and began to pray. A few others joined him, and Farhad knelt by himself on his sleeping mat, but most boys gathered at the other end of the room, poring over a crumpled section of the newspaper.

I sat on my mat, a thin piece of rubber between me and the concrete floor. My new home. No music, no clothes or anything else to call my own, no one who knew me. I should have left with Uncle that night. Dying with him in Tehran would've been better than this.

On the mat next to me, Jaafer motioned toward the group of boys. "They're talking football. The Cup games are almost over. I've been so out of it, I had no idea."

"I thought I was the only one who didn't know," I said, remembering how we'd talked of nothing but the games at the training camp. "We can't ask now; they'll think we're idiots."

"If we listen long enough, we'll figure it out. I had money on Italy, but even if I won, I can't collect." Jaafer leaned against the wall with his arms behind his head. "The guys I bet with were in front of me in the minefield."

I closed my eyes, hoping to clear the image of the fireball, but it brought back the screaming and the air-sucking whoosh of the explosions.

Jaafer sighed. "Definitely not the Hilton, but I was expecting worse, and like the man said, it's better than being in a trench." He yawned and stretched. "And it's better than being dead."

"I guess."

Jaafer looked over. "Oh, you're like that jerk at lunch? What was his name? Pasha? Totally pissed because he didn't croak? He's probably envious that his dead buddies are up in heaven, making out with the seventy promised virgins."

I smiled. My cheek muscles strained with the effort. "That's what my mother told me, but she skipped the part about the virgins."

"That's like my father. Wanted me to sign up the first week of the war," said Jaafer. "I was only eleven." He swatted at a fly that flew lazily around his head. "Mom made me wait until I was twelve. When my father left for the front, he slapped me on the back and told me he'd see me soon in heaven. I say bull."

"Be nice if we knew for sure," I said.

"Yeah, but there's only one way to know and I'd rather not be dead." Jaafer inclined his head in Pasha's direction. "I know his type. When we go home, he'll still be thinking he should've died."

"If they gave you a choice—home or back to the front—what would you do?" I asked.

Jaafer looked at me like I'd asked if he wanted to drink boiling oil.

"Home. No question. My mom needs me, especially if my father gets himself killed. I'm hoping I still have friends left when I get back. You?"

"My mother thinks I should be dead. If I go home, I'll be hearing about that daily. My father died at the beginning of the war and my uncle was killed in the resistance back in March. I don't know about my friend Ebi." I breathed in. I hadn't strung that many words together since Kamran left for the front.

"If not home, where would you go?"

I heard soft crying. For a second I thought it was me. But the sound came from the other end of the room, where Farhad was curled in a ball. I shifted, trying to get comfortable.

"I have no idea where I'd go," I said. In a rush, Uncle's words came to me: *Sometime, somewhere, there'll be a place where you can grow your gift.* I squeezed my eyes tight. If such a place existed, there was no road from here to there.

CHAPTER FOURTEEN

I wonder if the classroom has bars," I said to Jaafer as we walked to class after breakfast the next morning. "In all those great prison movies that used to be on TV, I don't remember any classrooms."

"I barely remember school that wasn't religious mumbo jumbo," Jaafer said. "If that's what these classes are, that's worse than being locked up all day."

The room was drab. Old desks and chairs were scattered in uneven rows. Walls that had once been white were gray with grime. When I stepped through the door, I blinked several times. Standing at the front of the small room was the oddest-looking man I'd ever seen.

His thick, unruly hair was red like a hot electric coil on a stove. And his skin! I'd never understood why they called white people white, but this man was just that. His skin was pale with spots of pink high on his cheekbones. He was large, not fat, but a foot taller than any boy in the room. He looked as if his shoulders would take up the whole doorway.

In three strides he stood in front of Jaafer and me, looking at a sheet of paper in his hands. "Hello, gentlemen. One of you is Reza and the other, Jaafer. Which is which?" We introduced ourselves.

"Welcome. I'm Miles O'Leary. Come in; find a seat anywhere and we'll get started." He spoke Farsi well, but with an accent I couldn't place.

"This morning we're having a class in French. Either of you take French in school?" We both shook our heads. "Well, everyone's at a different level here. You might be able to pick something up. We have other classes, too, lots of classes. After we're done this morning, we can talk. We can see what interests you."

I stole a glance at Jaafer as we sat down. We had a choice? Jaafer shrugged.

Even though I didn't understand a word, I liked the sound of French, especially the way this Miles O'Leary spoke. Like a song searching for a melody. I was surprised when the bell rang. An hour and a half had passed.

As the others left, Miles folded his arms and legs into a seat next to us. "Did you get any of that, gentlemen?"

"A little," said Jaafer. I nodded.

"How about other languages? Either of you speak any English or Arabic?"

"My aunt speaks English," said Jaafer. "She's tried to teach me."

"I had some of both in school, before the revolution," I answered.

"Good, good, we try to do English or Arabic at least once a week. Hopefully you can learn without picking up my odd accent." He smiled. "I'm from Belfast originally, in Northern Ireland, but I've lived in a dozen places. Well, at least a dozen places since I left school. Came from America—Boston—most recently. I butcher Farsi just like the four other languages I speak."

He smiled and pointed to a small stack of books and paints in the corner. "They actually let us try to have a decent school here. Sometimes we do pretty well. Right now we have four teachers roving between camps."

I wanted to stop him and ask about Ebi, but he was on a roll. "We teach literature and art here. In the room down the hall we teach . . ." He paused, scratching his forehead. "Oh, how do you say it? Wait . . . vocational, that's it . . . vocational skills—appliance repair, that kind of thing." He rubbed his hands together, clearly proud he'd found the right word. "At least once a week, I try to get in a music class."

I'd been looking down at the desktop, but my glance flew up like a strong magnet to lock with Miles's sky-blue eyes.

"Aha—what do we have here?" He chuckled. "A musician? What do you play, Reza?"

"No . . . nothing. Well, I used to play piano. But it got pretty hard after the revolution, so I don't really play now."

"Okay. All right. Do you sing, maybe?"

"A little." I could feel my cheeks getting hot. "Mostly I just like music."

Miles's face got brighter. "Great. I fancy myself a bit of a musician, too, and there aren't many of us here." He smiled at me. "What kind of music do you like?"

"My uncle was teaching me about jazz, but he died earlier this year."

"That's a shame. Really sorry." Miles shook his head and touched my hand. "At least you have family that'll let you listen. I have a friend from Tehran. He'd never heard anything, nothing, but religious music before he came to university."

"Actually, my mother doesn't allow music." I remembered

the sound of shattered plastic and saw my ruined tape player under a mess of tea leaves. "My uncle would sneak me stuff."

Miles's bright face darkened. "It's bloody ridiculous." He blew air out in a fast whoosh. "I try to respect cultural differences and all that, but think of it—the next Duke Ellington could be an eleven-year-old girl in Tehran and she'll never know. She's not even allowed to have that dream."

I moved back in my seat. Miles ran both hands through his hair and said, "Sorry, boys, you must think old Miles is a little mad, a bit unhinged, eh?"

Actually, I didn't think he was that old—probably about the same age as Uncle Habib. He didn't seem mad, either. Odd, but not mad.

"You just hit a sore point, that's all." He stood, putting his hands in his pockets. "Promise I'll be better behaved tomorrow. Go on now, it'll be lunch soon."

Leaving the room, I looked back over my shoulder at Miles packing up his books. As I walked into the bright sunlight I hummed an old folk song I hadn't heard for years. It had been one of Uncle's favorites.

*   *   *

We walked into the cafeteria and it smelled like we'd opened an oven door. Salar raised his voice to be heard over a hundred boys using metal spoons to fill metal bowls. "What do you think of Miles?"

"Bit of a lunatic," said Jaafer, frowning. "But he seems okay."

"Some guys don't like him 'cause he's white." Salar laughed. "White as rice pudding. But he's all right. Before he got here, we were half-dead from boredom. Plus, the guards don't mess with us when he's around."

"He's a jazz fan," I said. "Any Duke Ellington fan is good with me."

"Who's Duke Ellington?" asked Omid.

"American piano player from the fifties," I said. "Genius."

Pasha's head jerked up. His eyes shot an arrow of hate in my direction. "American? Piano?" His voice rose. "Is there no end to your blasphemy, ingrate?"

"Calm down, man," I said, holding my palms out in front of me as if I could stop his words. "I'm not asking you to listen. Just saying I'm a fan."

"Your music is cursed." Pasha stood above me in an instant. I rose to face him. All talking around us stopped. "Your God declared that music is cursed, tools of music are cursed, theaters and halls where music is played, they're cursed, too."

"I know what I'm supposed to think, Pasha." I took a step back. "All I'm saying is I know what I like." I locked eyes with him, weighing my next words. I probably shouldn't have said them, but in that moment the truth felt sweet in my mouth. "To me, it feels like the God I love made this music, too."

"What you feel," said Pasha in a mocking tone. "You'll be judged for what you feel."

Before I knew what happened, Pasha hooked a foot behind my ankle and yanked. I hit the cement floor. Hard. Instinctively, I reached and pulled Pasha down next to me. He grabbed my head in a choke hold. I flailed, trying to wrestle free, but before I could move away, four guards pulled us apart.

I smelled Abass before I heard him. "This new one hasn't been here two days and he's on the floor."

Before I could defend myself, Jaafer said, "He was only trying to—"

"Shut up, moron. I should lock all of you up—is that what you want?"

Abass gripped my arm. Another guard had Pasha. They dragged us to the far side of the cafeteria. We reached an empty table, and Abass shoved me roughly onto the metal bench. My spine rattled top to bottom when Pasha landed next to me.

"Do you think this is a playground? Pasha, you've been here long enough to know fighting isn't tolerated." Abass squeezed my arm tighter and tighter as he said this. I knew there'd be finger-shaped bruises by morning. "No wonder we're winning this war. We should just leave you to it and maybe you'd all kill each other."

In one swift motion, he let go of me and grabbed the club he carried on his belt and swung it quickly in front of our faces. "If I catch you out of line again, you'll wish you'd never met me."

I almost said *That's been true since I first smelled you*, but caught myself.

✳ ✳ ✳

The next morning I hurried to class to ask Miles about Ebi, but six boys were already clustered around him, talking excitedly.

When they saw me their conversation stopped. Miles glanced at them, then at me. "Here less than a week and already roughing it up? You gotta be careful, lad. Really gotta be careful."

"It wasn't his fault," said Salar. "Pasha attacked him, but old Fish Butt didn't see that."

"And besides," chimed in Omid, "Pasha's the guard's favorite."

As a stream of boys walked in the classroom, Miles said, "Sit down, gentlemen, sit down. I'd like to talk about this with all of you."

When everyone had settled in, Miles sat on his desk and tapped his fingers together. I felt worse than dirt. Miles reminded me of Uncle, and I'd already managed to disappoint him.

"As most of you know, I grew up in Belfast. I've seen

violence, but the minefields, the way most of you boys landed here, it's . . ." He looked like he was searching for a word. He held up both his hands and motioned toward us. "I know what I think about all this, but what about you, boys? Was the war what you expected?"

We all shifted around, stealing glances. I realized that Pasha wasn't in the room. I felt like Miles was talking directly to me.

Salar looked around. In the short time I'd known him he'd never been without a smile, but now his face was dark as a storm cloud as he said, "My family's pretty patriotic. All my uncles and cousins were going, so it seemed like I should go, too. I sort of wanted to fight, you know, like in the movies, but they didn't let us fight, did they?" He studied his hands.

Farhad's small voice came from the front of the room. "Hussain ibn Ali has always been my hero. I wanted to give my life for justice and truth like he did. When I woke up in the hospital and saw this"—he pointed to his stump—"I thought I'd failed. How could I have been stupid enough to get caught in a minefield the first day out?" His voice got even lower. "I felt like an idiot, but when I realized it happened to all of us, it made me feel better."

"They thought we were disposable," added Omid in his deep voice.

"I'd agree," said Miles. "It's an abomination against whatever God you believe in." He let his words hang in the air.

"I wonder what Pasha thinks," said Jaafer. "He talks big, like Khomeini can do no wrong, but sometimes he must feel like we do."

Farhad spoke up again. "I think he feels like I do. We came to be martyrs and were never given the chance. It makes him so angry." He paused for a second. "It only makes me sad."

"Interesting point," said Miles. "Could be why he lashes out." He was quiet then, as if waiting to see if we had anything else to add. "I have to be careful about what I say here, boys. I have some protection because I have friends in the press and in the Red Cross." He tapped his forehead. "I mean the Red Crescent; in Europe and America they call it the Red Cross. But even with that, the camp could send me packing if I say too much."

He moved to the first row of desks, his hands in his pockets, his voice a little lower. "Even though I have to be careful, I'll tell you what I think. I think you'll leave here either as strong men or broken boys—*that's your choice.* Learning to get along with one another, coming to class, reading, these things will spit you out strong. Fighting with each other—or even worse, with those guards—that'll break your spirit and your bones, too. You can come to me if you need to talk. I may not be able to help you, but I can listen for as long as I'm here."

Miles nodded twice and then clapped his hands together.

"All right, enough said, gentlemen. Let's get on with class; let's get moving. Today we're going to start in on something written by that geezer Shakespeare."

After class I lingered in my seat. I didn't want to face Miles, but I didn't want to walk away, either. Before I could decide what to do, Miles stood in front of me.

"Reza?"

"Yes, sir?"

"No need to call me sir. Miles will do. Miles is just fine. Something you need here this morning, lad? You don't want to be late for that wonderful food."

I took a deep breath. "Sir, I mean Miles, I . . . I guess I . . ." Another deep breath and I said, "Sorry about the fight yesterday."

"No worries, man. My little speech wasn't directed only at you. You're the latest one, but you aren't the first to be in the way of a fight."

He went back to the desk, putting his things in an old briefcase. "Also, you'll learn I can get a bit preachy, eh? I get carried away." He snapped his bag shut and motioned for me to join him. I walked slowly behind him.

Miles stopped at the door and turned. "Is there something else, son? Something else bothering you?"

Like a ball fast off my foot, the words came. "They say you

know everyone in camp and some in the other camps. Is that true?"

"*Everyone*—there's an exaggeration." Miles laughed, but stopped when he saw my face. "Well, try me."

"I'm looking for a friend who was in the minefield with me." I watched my shoes as if Ebi's new address might show up there. "His name is Ebi. Ebi Saberi."

Miles thought for a moment and shook his head. "Sorry, don't know him. But I'll keep my ears open." Miles waited until I looked up, then said, "You're afraid he's gone?"

I didn't move.

"I know it's hell, Reza. To see so many killed. But you survived. These camps are full of boys who survived. There are three other facilities in the north full of boys, too." He came and stood beside me, draping his long arm over my shoulders. "Have hope, man. It's all you can do."

CHAPTER FIFTEEN

I did my best to steer clear of Pasha as the days went by. I sat in the dusty yard, watching for clouds. The little piece of blue, squared off by concrete walls, seemed like the only sky I'd see for the rest of my life. I thought about home. Sometimes the image of Mother standing in the dusty street wouldn't leave me. Once I was surprised by a tune that surfaced from a place long forgotten, a tune that rested on the tips of my fingers and lightly played on my knee.

I looked forward to the music class Miles had promised, but

it wasn't scheduled the first few weeks. When the day finally came I woke with butterflies in the pit of my stomach—how I usually felt on the first day of summer. I hurried through breakfast to get to the classroom early.

"Take a seat, boys. We have good stuff to cover today, excellent stuff."

Miles talked about meter signatures—how many beats per measure in different kinds of music. He went through three-quarter time and four-quarter time. He beat the count with his hand on his desk. The guys around me yawned, but I listened with every atom. When the hour was almost up, I took a sharp breath, shocked. I hadn't thought of Ebi or Uncle since class started.

As he was finishing up, Miles clasped his hands and turned them over, cracking his knuckles. "Before I let you go, I'm going to sing you two songs, both ballads—one from my culture and one from yours. Listen to the differences and the similarities." He cleared his throat. "I'm not going to sing this in Farsi, but those of you who know a little English may be able to catch some meaning. It's an Irish battle song called 'Rising of the Moon.'"

It was the most lonesome group of notes I'd ever heard. Lonesome, but strangely comforting, too. I couldn't believe that such sad, sweet notes could come from this bear of a guy.

When Miles finished he didn't say a word, but immediately started singing my favorite ballad by Dariush Eghbali. Like the first song, the notes were sad and sweet, but in a completely different way. I hadn't heard this song since before the revolution. Aunt Azar and Uncle had sung it at the dinner table. I could almost smell Auntie's favorite spicy hot tea.

The combination of the music and the clear picture of Uncle Habib's smiling face made me press my palms against my eyes, pushing sandbags up against the memories that threatened to drown me.

As soon as the song was finished, I stood. I kept my head down and was first through the classroom door. In two steps I bumped into green boots and green pants. I forced myself to look up, dreading Abass's scowl, but it was the quiet guard I'd noticed near our lunch table. I quickly wiped my eyes and saw the small man looking at me through tears of his own.

For a second, our stare took up the space where the music had been. Then boys tumbled out of the room behind me, heading for lunch. The guard looked away and moved down the hall in the other direction.

* * *

At lunch I saw the same guard standing four tables over, staring straight ahead.

"Salar, what's the story with that guard over there?" I asked, tilting my head toward the man.

"The little guy?"

I nodded.

"That's Majid. Unlike most of these jerks, he's actually a human being. Abass is the worst of them, but they're all pretty nasty." He shrugged. "Majid sometimes seems to care what happens to us."

"Remember that time he slipped us all chocolate for no reason?" asked Omid.

I watched Majid. When our eyes met, I thought he'd look away, but I saw the flicker of a smile, like the flutter of a bird's wing at the edge of my vision.

I thought about how music could affect this guard and Miles the same way it did me. Logically it made sense that other people in the wide world would be infected by this disease, but in a way I wished it was unique, passed only from uncle to nephew.

* * *

It was the last week of Ramadan, and Pasha never seemed to move from his sleeping mat during the day. At dinner he was first at the table and heaped his bowl full of the watery stew—usually leftovers from breakfast and lunch with added rice.

On the final night of the week, the only seat left at dinner was next to Pasha. I thought about sitting at another table but decided not to let Pasha have that pleasure. I checked to make sure Farhad had a full plate, since he'd been fasting too, then I emptied what was left in the communal bowl into mine. Before I could take a bite, Pasha grabbed my bowl and poured it into his.

"What are you doing?" I asked, pulling at my bowl.

"I'm starving. You didn't fast today and I did. There's no more, so I'm taking yours."

"Did you think of asking?"

Our tussle brought three guards to the table. Abass swiped both bowls.

"What's going on here?"

"Pasha stole Reza's food," explained Farhad.

"Is that so?" Abass looked at me, then at Pasha. Neither of us said a word. "Then I suppose they can both go without." He stacked the bowls on top of each other and reached for the communal bowl.

"That's not fair," said Farhad and Omid at the same time, but a look from Abass as he walked to the kitchen made them swallow their words.

"Here, I have a few bites left." Omid passed me his bowl. "You can finish it."

"Thanks," I said. I left for a table nearby and ate the few bites in silence.

At the end of the meal, Abass came to line us up. Majid came out of the kitchen and said to Abass, "I'll keep the end of the line in order."

I glared at Pasha's back. When we moved through the door, Majid slipped me a small paper bag. Inside were a dozen dates— the sweetest dates I'd ever tasted.

CHAPTER SIXTEEN

J aafer and I leaned against the fence, watching the black-and-white ball pass from foot to foot. It'd been ages since my arm really hurt, but the idea of the pain was still fresh in my mind. Neither of us had played since we arrived.

"Come on," yelled Omid. "Get your butts over here."

"I guess it's time," said Jaafer. "We've been sitting on the bench too long."

I shrugged. We joined the game. I was surprised how good it felt to move, to reach my foot into a jumble and pull the ball out, the sound of it—*whack*—as it flew toward the makeshift goal. When I finally collapsed to catch my breath, Jaafer fell down next to me.

"Check it out. New recruits," he said, pointing to the guard station. I saw eight boys wearing clean yellow canvas spilling out of an old jeep. Abass motioned to Salar, who put on his tour-guide face and headed over.

I wandered over to the group. If they'd come from another camp, maybe they'd seen Ebi. Out of nowhere, Kamran's spiky head popped into my mind. Maybe he and Ebi were hanging out somewhere together. I felt a smile that didn't reach my lips.

A boy was talking when I came near. ". . . Yeah, I hear this is the best camp to be at. It's brutal where we were. Some guys were beaten and burned and others just disappeared—we never knew if they were shipped to other camps or something else."

"Rough," said Salar. "Hear that, Reza? You better hope he doesn't know anything about your buddy." He turned back to the new boy. "That's all Reza here cares about, finding his boyfriend."

"He's not my boyfriend." I lunged at Salar. He fended me off with a punch.

"Who is he?" asked the boy.

I told him Ebi's name and described him.

"Sorry, I don't know any Ebi."

"Like I said, you should be happy he's not at that camp." Salar clapped me on the back and motioned toward the class-rooms. "Come on. Let's show them around our humble home."

The boy's words—"others just disappeared"—lodged in my brain. Could Ebi have survived the minefield, only to be killed by some slimy guard? Sometimes Abass's scowl replaced the fireball that woke me in the middle of the night.

* * *

One night as we slept, winter strode into camp. Frost left lace tablecloths across the yellow dirt. We swatted the cloudy trails our breath left as we headed to breakfast and class.

When Miles walked into the room with an instrument case under one arm, a riff of happy notes twirled into my brain. He opened the case and carefully lifted out a skinny something with a long neck. I immediately thought of Dad's old guitar.

"You're in for a treat today, lads. I'm going to give it a go with an instrument that I just picked up—the tar. I found it at a secondhand shop on my day off. I can play guitar passably and I've messed around with a lute, so I thought I could handle this thing, but I'm still getting the hang of it. I wanted to play you Rumi. His music bloody begs for an old tar."

The word *Rumi* was like bait on a hook. Uncle's voice rang in my head: *Rumi was your kind of guy. . . . He was all about reaching God through singing and dancing.* I moved to the front row.

Miles fumbled to get the fingering right. When he looked up, his eyes met mine and sparkled like diamonds caught in the sun.

After two measures I knew the song. It was one Uncle had taught me when I was little. My father used to sing it, too, sometimes. At least before the revolution.

The oddness of Miles's accent faded as I listened to the words. Some of the phrases were old and strange, but others could have been pop lyrics. When Miles came to these words, I swallowed hard against the lump in my throat:

> *You have seen your own strength.*
> *You have seen your own beauty.*
> *You have seen your golden wings.*
> *Of anything less,*
> *why do you worry?*

The cold morning sun reflected off the frets as Miles's fingers moved up and down. I hadn't thought of the song in years, but when I was eight, this song made me feel strong and proud.

The notes faded away. There was something in the room that hadn't been there before—a scent of home, delivered by the old instrument. Miles let it linger for a minute before jumping into a lecture on music from other countries. Before class ended he strummed another melody, an old Celtic lullaby.

"That's enough for today, gentlemen," said Miles. "Better get to lunch. I've kept you a little long this morning. Don't forget, we have a special session this afternoon in watch repair. If any of you are interested, it'll be upstairs in Room Six."

Chairs scraped and desks clanked together as we left the room. Miles put the tar away and placed it in the corner.

I stared at the tattered black case. My fingers ached to open it—to feel the tar's wooden neck, to hear it sing under my touch. Miles walked out of the room, talking to Omid about something, but I wasn't listening. I couldn't tear myself away. It was like the last piece of honey cake. The polite thing would be to walk away, but the memory of sweet, sticky melodies made me take a step closer. Would I be able to play? Could I . . . ?

"I'd forget my head if it weren't screwed on." Miles burst back into the room. "I forgot to lock up. Anything I can do for you, Mr. Reza?"

My eyes flitted around the room, looking for a reason I might be standing there like a tree trunk. "No, ah, just going."

Miles slapped me on my back, dreams of cake and music scattered. "I need to lock up and you'd better get to lunch. It tastes like warm mud, but it'll keep you alive."

CHAPTER SEVENTEEN

As promised, Miles had invited an old man from town to spend two hours after lunch talking about the inside of a watch. It seemed like a boring idea to me, but several other guys had fathers and grandfathers who were jewelers. Over our lunch of gray lentils and overcooked onions, they talked about opening their own shops when they got home.

Even boys who never went to Miles's classes wanted to see a new face. By the time Jaafer and I had finished our lentils and walked into the waning winter sun, the yard was deserted except for a group in the far corner.

"I heard Borzin made a deal for a newspaper." Jaafer pointed across the yard. "He'll be cleaning the toilet for a month. Let's check the scores."

"You go ahead," I said, pulling my jacket close. "I'm gonna take a leak, maybe sit there awhile to stay warm."

"You're going to that stupid watch thing up in Room Six, aren't you?"

"No. I just don't want to freeze here for two hours. I'll be back in a while."

Laughing, Jaafer headed toward the group of boys. "Please yourself, but you'll have to pay me to tell you the scores."

"Yeah, right," I shouted back. I stepped into the dark hallway and walked directly to the classroom we'd been in that morning. The tar was calling me, calling so loud and clear it was a wonder no one else heard. I stood before the closed door.

Somewhere in my head I heard Uncle say, *Open the door, Cub. Nothing there to bite you.*

I reached for the knob. It didn't move. I was just about to turn away when I noticed a row of windows above the classroom door. The first one was ajar, and I wondered if I could get up there and fit through it.

I looked up and down the hall. Ten feet away was a rickety chair. Without making a sound, I picked it up and placed it below the window. Standing on the wobbly seat, I could just reach the windowsill. I gripped it with all my strength and hoisted myself up.

Twice I was able to get my head past the sill to peek in, but I couldn't pull my shoulders up. I stood on the chair and took a deep breath. Pulling again, I finally fit my shoulders through the opening and gently pushed until my waist rested on the windowsill.

Hanging above the room, I realized I was stuck.

It was at this exact moment that I heard a door open down the hall, followed by footsteps. It sounded as if someone was around the corner. They'd be on me in seconds. I thought of the diving board on the platform at the lake where I used to swim. The footsteps came closer. I tucked my head and dove.

After clattering to the floor, I lay in a ball. Could I have been any stupider? Even if the person connected to the footsteps hadn't seen my legs hanging out the window, he would have had to be deaf not to hear the racket.

I lay on my side, not moving, waiting for whoever it was to try the door. But no one came. It was silent in the hallway. I tensed my muscles and lifted my limbs, assessing the damage.

I'd instinctively protected the arm that I'd broken, but the other one would be bruised. Everything else seemed fine.

Who was out there? Maybe it was someone like me, sneaking around where he shouldn't. I gingerly got to my feet and moved to the door. Pressing my ear against the cold wood, I was distracted by my thumping heartbeat. I looked at the clock on the wall. Only ten minutes gone since I'd left lunch and the class upstairs had started. It felt like forever.

I froze again. Someone might come by and notice the chair under the window. Then I'd be screwed. I stood for another five minutes, willing myself to stop worrying.

The tar sat right where Miles had left it. I walked to the case and took it out. It smelled like the oil Grandmother used to polish her table.

Other than the piano, I'd hardly ever been close to another instrument. During the few times I'd played Dad's guitar I'd learned only a few chords. But when I settled the tar on my lap and smoothed my hand over the honey-colored wood, it felt like home. The double bowls were covered with thin membranes of stretched skin and were connected to a long neck holding six strings. I strummed and placed my fingers in different positions to change the sound. Then I lifted a pick from the case and tried it on the strings. The richness of the sound filled the room.

I strummed softly until I found chords that felt familiar. Watching Dad play when I was little had imprinted on me. The way a baby duck knows its mother, my fingers flew to the frets. After so many months, happiness was finally a thing I could touch.

I played quietly so the noise couldn't be heard outside the locked door, losing myself in the memories of the music. I was working my way through all the songs I could remember when I heard a door slam. Suddenly a horde of boys clattered down the stairs. I'd meant to stay for a few minutes, but almost two hours had flown by.

I put the tar back, pausing for only a split second to stroke the wood, warm from my lap. I crept to the door and peered through the keyhole.

Slowly opening the door a crack, I saw no one. I darted out, picked up the chair and put it back in its place. When I straightened, I heard a throat clearing behind me. Knowing I couldn't run, I took a deep breath and turned around. Majid leaned against the wall. The guard wore a slip of a smile. He must have been listening. He nodded, turned, and walked away.

The simple nod sent a gust of warm relief that traveled from my shoulders and down my spine. It weakened my knees ever so slightly. I stood perfectly still for a few seconds, enjoying the warmth. Then, knowing I'd be missed, I sprinted toward the yard but skidded to a stop before running through the door. It wouldn't look good to run out like I was being chased. I watched the yard until the lockdown bell was sounded. In the confusion of the boys moving around, I fell into step next to Jaafer.

"Where were you, man?" he asked when I joined the line beside him. "I thought Fish Butt might have locked you up or something."

"No." I looked around to make sure we were out of earshot. "I sneaked into the classroom to play that old tar. I lost track of time."

"What are you? Stupid or brave?" asked Jaafer. "I didn't know you could play."

A quick smile spread across my face. "Neither did I."

Jaafer knit his brow but let it pass.

As we walked to lockup, my head was a stew of dreams and memories. The sound track in my head was back, needing to be played. It was magic. Hearing music, playing music, made me think of Uncle. But for a few minutes, actually shaping the notes had taken me to a place where I might be happy for the rest of my life.

CHAPTER EIGHTEEN

here are you, Reza? Dreaming of some naked girl?"
Jaafer kicked the side of my leg harder than he needed
to as he slumped down next to me. "You've been staring off into
space for twenty minutes. Come to think of it, what's up with
you? You've been acting weird for days."

I shrugged and mumbled. The truth was, my fingers ached
to pick up the tar again. Ached more than I'd ever wanted nou-
gat candy or even a new tape from Uncle. We sat aimlessly, and

I half listened as Jaafer told me about this girl who lived on his street at home. I'd heard the story before, but I let him tell it again.

"Reza." Another kick from Jaafer.

"What?"

"I asked if you think she'll remember me. Man, the least you can do is pretend to listen."

"Sorry," I mumbled.

We both turned at the sound of a shout across the yard.

Two new kids were standing nose to nose, fists raised. One yelled something at the other, and in a flash they were rolling in the dust. Boys ran from every corner of the yard bellowing encouragement. Jaafer took off toward the fight, but I took a step backward.

I waited until I was sure the few guards patrolling were focused on the fight to make my move. Heading for the classroom door, I wondered if I was foolish enough to try the chair again. When I reached the hall I looked around. The old chair was gone. I tried the door. Locked. I slid down, rested my head on my knees, and stayed like that for a few minutes. Finally I pulled myself up, telling myself it was nothing, just a stupid old guitar. That I didn't care if I ever held it again.

I shuffled away from the room. Putting off the time I'd have to talk to Jaafer and the rest, I leaned against the gateway to the yard. The fight was over. Abass and another guard dragged the boys toward lockup. Majid stood a few yards away, the only guard left in the yard.

He caught my eye and looked away. As soon as the door shut behind Abass, Majid glanced quickly to his right and left, then turned and walked straight at me. As he passed he caught my eye for a fraction of a second, his eyebrows raised. What was that? I liked this guy, but he was a guard. Was I to follow him? He didn't look back. I watched him stride to the locked classroom door. Once there, almost before I could register what he'd done, he reached up to the ledge above the door and either took something or left something and then walked back to the yard.

He returned to the place he'd been, surveying the sea of boys. I was probably the only one who'd noticed he'd gone. That must have been the idea. I raced back to the door and jumped up to reach the place Majid's hand had been. Something clattered to the floor. A key—the key to the classroom door. I wanted to run out and hug him, jump up and down. But instead I used the key to open the door and spent forty minutes smiling—with the tar in my lap.

From then on I checked the ledge above the door as often as I could. The first two weeks after that day, I checked ten times, but the key was never there again. I worried that maybe I shouldn't have put it back. Maybe he meant for me to keep it, but that seemed too dangerous.

My eleventh try I swore would be my last. It was stupid to want something that wasn't ever going to be there. But it was there, the tar was mine for an hour, and I was home. From then on sometimes the key was there, mostly it wasn't, and every time I found it I felt like I'd won the lottery.

* * *

After breakfast one Saturday in mid-November, it was so cold, we begged Abass to let us go back to our room, where we could be out of the icy wind.

"Please, sir. You guys have those heavy coats and we have these . . ." Salar fingered his jacket, searching for a word. "I don't know what you call them, but you wouldn't call them warm. I look like a tulip in this thing."

"To the yard, all of you," Abass spat.

"Please," I asked, speaking directly to the guard for the first time. "By the time lunch comes, we won't be able to move our fingers."

Abass brandished the short club from his belt and waved it in the air. "Go."

Farhad whimpered and the rest of us hurried from Abass's dark glare. The yard was full of small groups huddled together, trying to keep warm. All the guards stood together near the office.

"Looks like everyone's on duty today. I wonder why," said Salar as Omid joined us.

Omid pointed to a group of boys standing near the office. "Those guys are being transferred to another camp. The jeep'll be here soon. The extra guards are just to make sure they go quietly. Nobody likes to leave Camp Six."

"I wonder where they're going," said Jaafer. "The guy who came from that camp up north, he was telling me the guards there use electric prods on their ears and tongues and worse places. He has burn scars on the bottoms of his feet."

I rubbed my hands together, trying not to picture Ebi being tortured. Then suddenly I felt like a light bulb turned on in my head. "Another camp?" I said. "I didn't know you could get transferred from here."

"What are you going to do, Reza? Tag along to find your friend?" Salar mocked. "Give it up, man. We all have friends dead or locked up somewhere around this country. You're not likely going to find him until we get home. And remember what they say about the other camps. This *is* the Hilton compared to those hell pits."

"I don't know," I said, watching the boys preparing to go. I squared my shoulders and looked straight at Salar. True, everyone had friends lost or scattered, but it seemed like these guys all had a mother or a father or an uncle caring about them, waiting for them at home. I had no one but Ebi. Without breaking my gaze I said, "I feel like I need to find him. Does anyone have paper and a pen?"

Salar laughed but handed me a stub of a pencil from his pocket. Jaafer gave me a scrap of paper from our English class the day before. I wrote both Ebi's name and my own three times on the small paper and tore them quickly. I palmed the three scraps and walked fast toward the group waiting near the office. Choosing three boys I knew slightly from Miles's class, I asked them to be on the lookout for Ebi.

"If you hear someone quoting Kojak, that'll be Ebi."

The boys laughed, then quickly pocketed the scraps of paper as Abass appeared.

"Move along, scum. You have no business with these ladies." The boys opened their mouths in protest, but Abass silenced them with a look. He shoved my shoulder hard and said, "Get back to your group."

I staggered a few steps and turned back. Making sure Abass couldn't see, I waved to the departing group.

When I rejoined our huddle, Jaafer said, "Weird. We'll probably never see them again. Or maybe I'll run into one of them in twenty years, in the bazaar, on my way home from work. I'll be buying dinner for my family of six, and one of them will be there selling jam."

Omid, shivering, thrust his hands into his armpits and said, "Assuming we're out of here in twenty years."

"I'm thinking positive." Jaafer laughed, then lowered his voice. "But, for real, one of the guys that came in yesterday heard that some aid group, maybe the Red Crescent, is trying to negotiate to get us sent home."

Salar crowed softly. "The Red Crescent is good! I could be home to help with my mother's spring cleaning." He rubbed his arms vigorously and stamped his feet. "I've got a game we can play instead of freezing to death. I call it Where's My Girlfriend? Pasha, why don't you start?"

Pasha glared at each of us in turn and said, "I'd have many girlfriends in heaven if I'd died like I was supposed to." He turned his back.

"I should have known better than to invite you to the party," said Salar. "I, then, will take the privilege of going first."

"You don't have a girlfriend," said Omid.

"If I hadn't been so stupid, signing up for this vacation spot, my next-door neighbor Havva would be my girlfriend by now. So, I'll play Where Is Havva? Salar paused, his gaze far from the dusty yard. "She's probably shopping. She and her mother go every Sunday morning. I can see her long, dark hair moving like . . ." Salar's voice failed as he waved his hand back and forth, caressing the air.

Pasha stood on the edge of the group, sneering. "You fools," he grunted. "You will never ascend to be with God. I should feel sorry for you, but I don't." He turned and walked to the other side of the yard.

We all watched him go. "Salar, long hair? Really? When was the last time you saw her without her chador?"

Salar shrugged and raised his eyebrow at the same time. "She hasn't cut it. The way she walks, I know her hair is swinging against those hips." He sashayed over to Omid, flipping the imagined hair over his shoulder. He put an arm around Omid's waist and nudged his hip. "And her eyes." Salar looked at Omid dreamily. "Those eyes go right to my soul."

"Get off, man." Omid pushed him away. "Your soul? More like your crotch." He made a grab below Salar's belt.

Salar ducked to escape and said, "Your turn, Omid. Oh, never mind. With that face, you'll never get a girlfriend."

"I *have* a girl, and I get to see her without her chador all the time."

"In your dreams." I laughed.

"Yeah, your wet dreams," sniggered Jaafer.

"Shut up." Omid lunged at both of us. Then he took a torn wallet from the pocket of his canvas pants and held out a tattered picture. He handed it around. "This is Ghodsi. Our parents are friends. When we visit, no one wears a chador." He looked at the picture as if memorizing her face, then said, "Where is she now? She could be with my little brother. Sometimes she takes care of him while my mother shops."

All the boys watched Omid; smiles flickered across their faces and were gone. Omid shook his head as if to break a spell and said, "Reza, how about you? A stud like you must have a girl."

"Where is she now?" I cocked my head, looking thoughtful. "Ah . . . she might be . . ." I started slowly and then sped up. "She lives in my building, so she might be visiting my mother. Sometimes she helps cook—you know, kissing up to my mom." I paused, while Jaafer watched me with a face full of questions. Softly, I finished. "She might be playing the guitar. Sometimes, if we're quiet so no one else in the building can hear, my mom lets us play for her."

The game went on, each of us taking his turn at spinning stories, until the lunch bell rang.

"What was that?" whispered Jaafer as we walked across the yard. "I thought your mom wouldn't allow you to play music, and how come you've never mentioned the girl?"

I smiled. "I made her up. I made up the guitar. And best of all, I made up a mother who'd let me play."

"Good one." Jaafer nodded, draping his arm over my shoulders as we entered the lunchroom. We all ate in silence, remembering fragrant kitchens and fleeting pictures of the lives we'd left behind.

CHAPTER NINETEEN

My feet landed in the same place every day—mat to the latrine, latrine to the yard, yard to the cafeteria, and back again. I remembered Ebi's boasting about how exciting life was going to be when we joined up. Never in my wildest dreams could I have imagined this kind of boredom.

Some weeks we saw Miles on Monday and then not again until Friday. On those weeks, by Friday I was like a junkyard dog, itching for class to begin.

"Take your seats." Miles perched on the edge of his desk.

He held a small tape player, and I thought again of the smashed machine in our kitchen. "I have different music for you today. Some of you might like this bloke. His name is Keith Jarrett, and he's an American, but he's much more popular in Europe than in the States."

Miles pushed play, and we listened to the sound of a lone piano. Someone staged a loud snore, but the music made me think of sitting on the front steps of Ebi's apartment house late one night, watching the empty streets and hearing the city fall asleep.

Farhad and I walked out together. He was shaking his head.

"What's up?" I asked.

"It's confusing. I know what the holy men say about Western music. I've always believed it, but I don't see how this stuff's going to hurt anyone."

"I don't get it either, my friend," I said.

The melody stayed in my head. We had an hour before lunch, and I could feel the frets of the tar under my fingers. I wanted to see if I could play the notes while they were still in my head.

When Miles crossed the yard on his way to the office, I looked around for Majid. He was watching me and gave me an almost imperceptible nod.

I gave an equally subtle bow in thanks. I think the key was warm to my touch when I pulled it from above the door. Once in the room, I took the tar in my lap and played. I hummed the tune over and over, my fingers so happy to move up and down the neck. I couldn't re-create the complexity of the piano music, but I quickly found the melody.

I kept playing, my body so connected to the tar that I didn't hear the key in the lock until the doorknob turned. Holding my breath, I watched the door open, and before I could exhale, Miles stood in front of me.

"What are you doing here?" Miles looked at the key in his hand and back at me. "How did you get in here?"

I thought about lying, but Miles deserved the truth. "I snuck in months ago. The guard, Majid, you know him?"

Miles nodded.

"He found me. I think he likes to listen outside the door, so he leaves the key above the door when he can." I looked down at my hands. "Sometimes. Not that often."

"Whoa." Miles blew out his lips. "You could both land in it deep for that one, deep indeed." He fell into a chair across from me. "But, Reza, it sounded splendid. Really amazing. That was the Jarrett tune you were playing, yes?"

"Trying to."

Miles raked his fingers through his wiry hair. "I thought you said your parents wouldn't let you play."

I strummed. "I played piano before the revolution, but I'd never played the tar before you brought it to class."

Miles leaned forward. "Let me hear that again. Play me that melody."

I played. It wasn't perfect, but in parts I felt the lonely heart of the song. When I was finished, I rested my hands on the neck and looked up shyly.

"That's unbelievable. Let me get this right: You've never played the tar before—"

"When I was younger, I picked up my dad's guitar once or twice, but other than that . . ."

"Yeah, well, you've barely played, you sneak in here for a month or two, and now you can play like that?" Miles stared at the tar. "You have a talent. A real talent."

"I used to *live* for music. I had tapes. . . ." My voice caught in my throat, and I couldn't finish the sentence.

"I remember. Your uncle. Your uncle who died, right?"

I nodded.

"What was his name?"

I moved my fingers silently over the frets. "His name was Habib."

Miles laid his big hand on my shoulder. "Your uncle would be proud. He would be very proud."

I met Miles's eyes. "I'm happy when I play. I haven't been anything close to happy since Uncle was killed. I'd stopped hearing songs in my head. I only heard noise, but now they're back. I . . ."

I faltered and turned my face back to my fingers. I hadn't meant to say so much. I took a breath and added, "Thanks for bringing in the tar."

When there was no response, I looked up. Miles nodded slightly and wiped his eye. He cleared his throat. "This is why I do this work, Reza. I'm so glad it spoke to you." He reached over and tapped the instrument. "I'm a little like you. Can't imagine my life without music. It must have been so hard to live in a place where you couldn't play or listen."

I nodded and we sat quietly for a minute.

Then Miles stood and opened his briefcase on the desk. "You better get to lunch." He reached into a pocket of his case. "But before you go, I want you to have this. Makes it a little easier to sneak in here. I'll tell Majid. Less risky for him, too."

I looked at the single key shining in my hand.

This was my key to heaven, not the plastic token I'd thrown in the hospital wastebasket.

CHAPTER TWENTY

I paid attention to the new transfers. As the weeks passed, fourteen slips of paper with my name and Ebi's written side by side left the camp. I checked with every incoming group. One day in the middle of winter a new group gathered by the office. I headed their way as soon as I saw them.

"Welcome to our home away from home," I said. "What camps have you guys come from?"

"Camp Twelve. Up north," said the oldest-looking boy.

I barely heard the response before I asked, "Any of you come across a friend of mine at your camps?"

One of the boys pointed at me and said, "Hey, crooked nose, slightly large ears, you must be Ebi's mate." He turned to another boy and asked, "What did Ebi say? Call him Maggot or something?"

A current spread through me like fire to paper. For a second it was as if all the air and all the sound was gone from the yard. A thousand thoughts raced through my mind in the time it took to breathe. Ebi was alive! At a northern camp, but he was alive! More than anything, I wanted to talk to him, to see his familiar face.

"Say that again?"

"Ebi told us to call you Maggot." I didn't even care about the Maggot part; I treasured the old insult. I grabbed the new boy and lifted him into the air. I put him down and danced around like I was possessed.

Jaafer came up behind me. "What the hell is going on, Reza?"

I picked him up, too, and danced him around in a circle. "Ebi! Ebi's alive!"

Jaafer laughed. "That's great, but put me down, you idiot."

I did, then turned back to the boy who knew Ebi. "Tell me about him. How is he?"

But before the boy could answer, Abass strode toward us, raising dust with every step.

"You," he said. "Why do I always find you near our new guests? If I catch you again, I'll . . ." He poked his dirty finger hard into my chest.

I caught myself from falling backward and stepped toward Abass.

"I was just talking to these guys, sir." I added the *sir* through clenched teeth.

"What do you have to talk about?" Abass was so close, I had to look up. The smell of him, his breath, his clothes, made my eyes water.

The new boys backed away. I saw them but couldn't focus. I sensed groups of boys all around me going silent.

I narrowed my eyes and glared at the big guard. Without warning, Abass grabbed my collar and pulled me off my feet. "I could send you away, you soft little Iranian," he jeered.

I struggled to get free. "And be away from you?" I croaked. The happy had turned to anger just as wild. "Make it happen, old man." As soon as I said it, I couldn't believe I'd let the words out of my mouth.

Abass tightened his grip on my collar and raised his fist. Just as he was about to hit me I felt someone grab me from behind. It was Miles. He pulled me away with one arm and held Abass back with the other.

"Enough," he said.

Abass stepped close to Miles. They were face-to-face, less than a foot apart. "He was—"

"I don't care," Miles interrupted. He released me and turned to Abass. "There is no need to hurt the boy."

"He—"

"Abass, I'll say it again. There is no need to hurt him. And it would not do to have him transferred." Then his voice was lower so only Abass and I could hear. "And you know I can report this."

"But, Miles," I interrupted. "My friend Ebi . . ."

Miles didn't look at me but said, "We'll discuss it later." He kept his eyes on Abass, as if staring down the barrel of a gun.

Finally Abass turned away, calling, "You new boys—with me."

"All right, Reza." Miles's hand covered my shoulder and steered me toward the lunchroom. "What say I join you boys for lunch today?" He swept his big arm toward the gape-mouthed crowd around us. "Come on, gentlemen, join us. Nothing to see here."

"But, Miles, I need to talk to those guys. My friend Ebi is alive."

"Later, Reza," Miles said. "Those new boys are with Abass

now and you will stay away." He quickened his pace. "It's been a while since I came to lunch. Onions and rice still the specialty?"

As soon as we sat down, Miles asked mundane questions about everybody's hometown. It was clear he didn't want to talk about what had just happened. One by one, the others answered hesitantly, stealing questioning glances at me when Miles wasn't looking.

My head was a boxing ring—elation and anger in opposite corners. I wanted to dance because Ebi was alive, but my fists clenched with rage when Abass brought the new boys in and glared in my direction.

"All right, I know all about where you're from, but how about family?" Miles stopped long enough to take a bite of rice. "Salar, do you torment brothers or sisters at home?"

"Yes, indeed, I do, sir," said Salar with a slight smile. "Two of each, all under ten."

"I might have known," said Miles.

"And you?" asked Salar. "Why aren't you married with a bunch of kids already?"

The corners of Miles's mouth went up slightly. "I was almost married. Right before I came here, as a matter of fact. To a beautiful girl named Myra."

"What happened?" asked Jaafer. "Did she leave you for another guy?"

"No." Miles looked from one to the other. "Not that simple. She left me for another life."

"Another life?" asked Omid.

"We planned to marry, then work with an international health organization in Africa before we settled back home. But she decided the two-year commitment was too long. Her dad offered to buy us a house straight off if we gave up the idea. I wasn't ready for that. Seems she was."

"Maybe she'll be waiting when you go back," said Jaafer.

"No luck on that." Miles smiled again. "I got a note from a mate that she was married last month. To a bloke who works in Daddy's company, no less."

I hadn't said a word since we left the yard. Miles caught my eye, but I looked away and pushed back from the table a few inches. Jaafer pressed on. "Do you have family back home?"

"My mother and two brothers." Miles reached in his pocket. He flipped open his wallet and tossed out a picture of a small red sports car.

"There's my real baby."

Salar grabbed the photo. "No way. That's a Frogeye Sprite. What year—'58?" The boys crowded around the picture.

"Pretty good guess. It's a 1960. How did you know?"

"My cousin had one before the revolution. I rode in it once." Salar made a roaring sound in his throat. "Does it run?"

"Like a top. That's if my mates are taking care of it like they promised."

While the other boys passed the picture around, I watched. Miles sat back and cocked his head to the side. "You're quiet, Reza."

"I guess I should thank you for backing him off."

Miles shrugged.

"But I'm wondering what would happen if I did get transferred. Maybe I could find Ebi."

"Reza, you don't want to go north. This is no summer camp, but conditions in those camps are wicked on a good day and dangerous on most. I can't tell you boys enough how lucky you are that you ended up in this camp." He scratched the back of his head and looked at all of us. "Haven't you noticed what a show they put on for the journalists when they come through?" The guys all nodded.

"They want the world to believe they're running a fine school, a prep school for young men. In their eyes, I help maintain that image. I'm a teacher, not just an aid worker."

"Is that why Abass didn't hit you when you got between him and Reza?" asked Salar.

"Probably." Miles steepled his hands under his chin. "They also know that I know people. People in the aid world, people at the paper in Baghdad. I have a few friends in the Red

Crescent. My friend Masood is stationed in Baghdad with them, just a hundred and eighty kilometers away. That's the only reason I have a little power around here. Remember, I've been to the other camps. You don't want to be there."

"Maybe I need to be there to help Ebi," I said.

Salar laughed. "Rez, you're a tough guy, but remember who you are. It's not like you can go in armed. Plus, there is no guarantee you'd get sent to the same camp."

"Salar's right," said Miles. "You can only hope he's one of the lucky ones who get transferred. I know it's hard, Reza. But what I'm saying is you have it easy here. Or at least you did. You didn't make a friend of Abass today. You'll need to watch yourself."

"Fish Butt hates everyone," said Omid. "I'd always wondered why he seemed sort of afraid of you, Miles. But he has a club, and all the guards around the wall have guns. Even if you do know people, aren't *you* afraid of him sometimes?"

"A man who lives to torment boys is not a brave man, not brave at all. I know that, and it's part of the reason he's afraid of me."

"That won't help if he decides to use that club on you," said Jaafer.

"He won't beat me, not me. I'm not afraid of that." Miles

rubbed the back of his neck. "I can't piss them off too badly, though, boys. I don't want to get sent home. If I make too much of a pest of myself, they'd find another freckled face to show the world."

"Have you talked to your Red Crescent friend lately?" asked Omid. "Are the rumors true that we might get sent home?"

"I've heard the rumors, too, but I don't know anything for sure."

Jaafer nodded toward the photo. "Wouldn't you rather be at home with your friends and your Sprite?"

Miles retrieved the picture, looking at it fondly. "I'll get back to it before too long. Soon enough." He put the picture back in his wallet. "It's different for me. Not the same. I didn't go through what you lads did to get here. Besides, who would torment you with bloody weird music if I weren't around?"

We all laughed, and the conversation moved on to sports cars we'd like to have. I couldn't stop thinking about Ebi.

Miles took another helping. When he'd eaten the last spoonful, he said, "Gentlemen, I have an idea I want to run by you. I want your advice. I've been thinking about organizing a play, you know, with costumes and music." He looked directly at me. "It might be a distraction for you all. What d'ya think?"

"Would it be allowed?" asked Jaafer.

"Don't know, won't know unless we try. Thought I'd check with all of you first. No use sticking my neck out if you aren't interested."

"What play would we do?" asked Farhad.

"You all know *One Thousand and One Nights*, yes? We could adapt one of those stories. How could anyone object to that? Write your story in Arabic and Farsi so no one can complain."

The lockdown bell rang and Miles stood up. He rested his hand on my head for a second. "See you in a few days, boys. Stay out of trouble until I get back."

CHAPTER TWENTY-ONE

During that long locked-up afternoon, we lay on our mats watching dust dance in the shafts of sunlight that moved across the room. The room was exactly the same as it had been when I'd left that morning, but now it felt less like a prison because Ebi was alive. As the fact sunk in, I thought about the fight with Abass. If he sent me away I'd never see Miles and the tar again. I replaced the thought with Ebi's grin.

"What do you guys think of Miles's idea? You know, doing

a play." I sort of liked the idea. But I wasn't going to let on that I did unless the other guys were in, too.

"It would pass the time, I guess," said Omid as he played with a scrap of paper he'd wadded into a ball. "Unless we're too old to put on a stupid play."

Salar stood up and paced. "It doesn't have to be a kids' play. Remember last year when those guys from that other camp came to play classical music for us? They were treated like they were on tour."

"Yeah, like Miles said, I bet they were rolling them out for the press," said Jaafer.

"Probably," agreed Salar. "But I talked to one of them when they were here. They got good meals at every camp they visited."

"Wait," I said as fireworks went off in my brain. "They had guys tour from another camp?" If we did a play and it had the possibility of getting me within shouting distance of Ebi, I had to do everything I could to make it happen.

Jaafer laughed. "Reza officially has a good reason for doing this play. He could find his friend Ebi, kidnap him, and bring him back to live with us."

I laughed back. "That's the ultimate plan, but I'd settle for seeing his face. And like Omid said, it'd pass the time. Any of those old stories have pirates in them? You'd make a good pirate, Jaaf."

"Most of those stories have people in prison. At least we could relate to that," said Jaafer.

"What about genies?" I sat up. "That three-wishes crap. We could wish for the Red Crescent to come out of a magic bottle and set us all free."

"We can't be too obvious with the prison thing," said Omid, throwing his paper ball for me to catch. "If it's too political, we'd get Miles in trouble."

We spent an hour discussing our favorites from the ancient stories, each telling the different versions we grew up with. Even Pasha joined in.

"I've got a good one," I almost shouted when the inspiration came. "How about *The Fisherman and the Genie*? No princesses. Salar wouldn't have to play the girl."

Salar threw his jacket in my direction.

"I don't remember that one," said Farhad.

"Sure you do," said Omid. "The fisherman pulls weird things up in his net, like a dead donkey and shards of glass. Then he pulls up this sealed copper jar."

"Right," chimed in Salar. "There's a genie in the jar who's royally pissed off because he's been there for four thousand years. Instead of granting wishes to whoever frees him, he lets the guy choose how he's going to die."

"Then the fisherman tricks him and gets him back in the jar. But I forget—did the guy ever get a wish?" Omid asked.

"No, there's something about magic fish the fisherman sells to the sultan for tons of money," said Salar.

"Oh, yeah, the fish," said Omid. "I was worried there wouldn't be parts for Jaafer and Reza."

I threw the paper ball back at Omid's head and Jaafer wrestled him to the ground while everyone cheered them on, but as soon as they were done, we started casting the play for real.

✵ ✵ ✵

That night it felt colder than ever. We tucked our thin blankets around us, wondering if the buildings were heated at all.

After a few minutes Jaafer said, "I wish Miles could find out more from his friend in the Red Crescent about us going home."

"I wonder if we'd all be able to go." I didn't like the thought of going home without Ebi. And, I realized, I didn't like the thought of leaving Jaafer here, either.

After a minute Jaafer said, "You were lucky Miles was there today, Rez. That jerk could have hurt you bad."

"All I could think about was getting to Ebi. It was stupid, but Abass is just another idiot, like those bastards that sent us through the mines."

Jaafer pulled his blanket up to his chin. "I'm just saying you should be careful."

I smiled in the dark. "I will be—and thanks, Jaafer." I waited for a response but realized that my friend was already asleep.

I woke up several hours later, wondering how I'd been asleep at all when it was so incredibly cold. Then I realized I'd woken because the key was turning in the lock. I didn't think it was possible to get colder, but a chill shook my already-frozen skin. The dim light coming through the high window shone on the door creeping open. Should I wake the others? I stifled a gasp when I saw Abass. I thought of the stories we'd heard of boys taken away and never seen again.

Before I could react, Abass walked down the length of the room holding something in his hand. What was it? It was too big for a gun. When he reached the far wall, I saw it was a step stool. What could he possibly be doing?

Keeping my eyelids almost closed, I watched Abass use the stool to reach up and open the windows as wide as they would go. Immediately a rush of frigid air filled the room. He opened all the windows he could reach.

The minute he left the room, I sat up and pulled my knees to my chest to conserve what little heat I had. Within a few minutes, the others started waking. Jaafer was the first to speak.

"What the—? Who opened the windows?"

"Abass," I whispered.

"We'll freeze to death," said Salar. "Can't we close the stupid things?"

"He had a step stool. Guess what? He didn't leave it for us."

"Jerk," said two boys at once.

Salar stood up and looked around. "Maybe someone could get on Omid's shoulders."

"Why me?" said Omid. "You're almost as tall as I am. Hey, Pasha, come here. Aren't you taller than I am?"

Pasha just pulled his blanket tighter around him and faced the wall.

"Come on, Omid. Stop arguing," urged Salar. "We need every inch we can get."

"If you can lift me up," said Farhad, "I bet I can get them."

Finally, after several tries, Omid and Farhad pulled some of the windows halfway shut, but the room was still full of our frozen breath. No one slept.

"It's my fault," I said.

"Forget it. The man's a moron," said Jaafer. "If it wasn't you, it would've been someone else."

"Probably me," said Omid, rubbing his hands together.

"One thing," said Salar as he yanked his blanket tighter

180

around him. "Tomorrow we don't give him the satisfaction. We'll pretend we slept like babies. We'll file into breakfast like it's the first day of summer. Agreed?"

Through chattering teeth, we all grunted agreement.

* * *

Salar was right. Acting cheerful the next morning made us feel surprisingly good. Especially when Abass scowled in our direction as we laughed and ate.

Jaafer, Omid, and I checked on the new boys after breakfast.

"If it isn't the Maggot," said the boy who knew Ebi. "You put on quite a show for our welcome—thanks."

"Aim to please," I said. "So you guys know Ebi?" I tried to keep my voice from squeaking.

"He came in a few months ago," said a younger boy. "At first he was pretty quiet, but I guess that's to be expected, given the circumstances."

I wondered what he meant, but then remembered my time in the hospital.

"A few weeks ago guys from here came into camp and had your name written on a piece of paper," said the older boy. "Ebi went wild. Singing and yelling your name. Come to think of it, he got clocked by one of the guards, too."

181

"Is he okay?"

The boys looked at each other. "He got banged up pretty bad, but he's all right, considering. Made us promise on our mother's soul that we'd look for you if we got here."

"Thanks," I said. "Wish I could see him, but at least I know he's alive."

Omid clapped me on the back. "Thank God we've got that figured out, right, chump?"

"Yeah." Jaafer nudged my ribs. "Maybe now we can talk about something else around here."

I smiled and kicked them both from behind.

CHAPTER TWENTY-TWO

B y the next music class, Miles had good news. The major who ran the camp had approved the idea of a play, telling Miles he always goes to the theater in his hometown.

"Of course, he still needs to approve the script, lads. Let's stay away from religion and politics. Think you can do that?"

The room erupted into chatter, and a sea of hands shot in the air, vying for Miles's attention.

"All right, boys. Stop your blather now. One at a time, please.

First, Salar—you expressed some interest in writing a script, yes?"

"At your service, sir." Salar bowed low. "It would help if I could get my hands on a copy of the original story. And can we get costumes? Maybe some scenery?"

Miles moved to his desk for a piece of paper. "Okay, give me a list. I'm going to Baghdad tomorrow. I'll do what I can, but I can't promise anything."

Miles came back a few days later with several boxes. Fabric. Paper. Paints. It was an odd assortment of things begged and borrowed, but it felt like a treasure chest. As we pored through the loot, Miles pulled me aside.

"I'd like you to be music director, Reza. Do you read music?"

"No. I just play what I hear, I guess."

"That's fine. You've obviously got an ear. I should be able to teach you the basics fast." He handed me two tattered books of sheet music. "You can help me choose the songs to go with the story, then you can direct the others who play. Will you do that?"

He wanted me to be in charge of the music? I'd never done anything like that. I couldn't imagine it. I started to give back the tattered books. But then, for a fraction of a second, I felt Uncle behind me. I pulled the books to my chest. I *could* learn to read music. I *could* play with other people. To be a real musician was all I'd ever wanted.

I straightened my shoulders just a little, tucked the music under my arm, and said, "I'll give it a go."

For the next few days Salar spent lockdown on his mat scribbling away. Sometimes he'd read us a passage and ask for help. Other times he'd tell us to shut up so he could concentrate. Finally the script was ready to go to the major. Miles promised he'd do what he could to get the major's quick approval, but days went by with no word.

Meanwhile we listened keenly for any talk of the Red Crescent's efforts to get us home. Rumors of a peace treaty sent a ripple of anticipation through the camp. Whenever we could, we'd get someone to translate articles from the local papers. Sometimes we'd get papers in Farsi, but the news was all of fierce battles without a mention of peace. The pictures always reminded me of our first day out—those stacks of dead bodies.

"Look at this," crowed Pasha, waving a battered old newspaper in the air at lunch one day. "Our leader will hold fast against talk of surrender." He read out loud: *"There are no conditions. The only condition is that the regime in Baghdad must fall and must be replaced by an Islamic Republic."*

"Idiot, a peace treaty isn't a surrender," I said. "It's more like a truce. Don't you know the difference?"

"There is no difference," growled Pasha. "There is nothing short of full victory."

"And meanwhile we'll be stuck here until we're old men." I snorted.

"It's worth the sacrifice."

I opened my mouth to reply, but Jaafer caught my eye. I sighed and turned away. Jaafer was right. Challenging Pasha was like building a sand castle at the water's edge. Nothing to show for the effort.

As we sat, Pasha put the paper on the table. I pulled it toward me and read.

Omid went to get the table's ration of rice and onions. Within seconds he hurried back with two huge bowls. "We're in luck. Rice and real meat today. Check it out."

Salar whistled softly. "What's up with this? Better be careful, boys—think they're trying to poison us?"

Everyone laughed weakly. I looked toward the door. "The food's not for our benefit, gentlemen. We get to eat it, but it's for show. Must be journalists."

We turned to see a group of men walk into the cafeteria with the major. Omid served the food. "I don't care why it's here. I'm going to enjoy it." He passed the bowls around the table.

"Look how puffed up the major is," said Jaafer through a full mouth. "Like a stupid peacock."

We watched as the men sat down to eat. Miles came into the cafeteria and joined the group. Two of them—one looked European and the other Iraqi—stood up to greet him with hugs and backslapping. After a few minutes of talking, Miles motioned them over to our table.

"Boys, meet my mates, Mark and Masood from the Red Crescent." As Miles introduced each of us, the major hurried over with the rest of the delegation. It was clear he hadn't planned for this meeting.

"Ah, yes, what have we here?" The major looked between Miles and the visitors. "Well . . . yes, this is our little group of thespians. As we speak, they are working on a play to perform for the rest of the camp."

Miles turned to face the major. "Excellent, sir. I assume that means you approved our script. The boys have been so anxious to hear."

"Ah . . . I . . ." The major faltered with the eyes of the delegation on him. "But, of course, it's a fine script. I very much look forward to seeing it performed. And maybe now we should move on, gentlemen."

"Excuse me, sir." Where did Jaafer get the guts to speak to the major? "I was wondering, sir, if we could ask our guests about the rumors we've heard that we might be sent home soon."

"Of course, I'd be happy to have you ask," said the major, though the furrows in his forehead said something different.

The man Miles had introduced as Masood looked at his colleagues, then back at the table. "I'll be honest with you. We don't know what's going to happen. It's very complicated, but there are a lot of people trying to negotiate on your behalf. All we can do is hope."

"Thank you, sir," said Jaafer, echoed by the rest of us.

"All right, well, I know we've all enjoyed our little visit, but we have much to see now," said the major. "Miles, will you take us to the classrooms?"

As they left the room, Miles looked over his shoulder and winked at us. After they were gone, everyone spoke at once. We laughed and clapped Jaafer on the back.

"We may really be going home, Rez," said Jaafer, his eyes shining. "Promise to come visit me."

"Absolutely." I nodded.

"Man, a little more enthusiasm would be nice."

"Jaaf, you have a family to go back to. If Ebi doesn't make it home, it's just me and my mother, who doesn't want me around."

"Come on, Rez. How do you know that?"

I reached over and grabbed Pasha's copy of *Ettela'at*. It was the newspaper my mother read. "Look at this." I read aloud: *"There is not a single school or town that is excluded from the happiness of waging war, from drinking the exquisite elixir of death or from the sweet death of the martyr, who dies in order to live forever in paradise.*

"My mother could have written this. If I'd come home a hero, it might have been different, but now she won't want me around as a constant reminder that I didn't die when I should have."

Jaafer took the paper and read it over again himself. "Isn't there someone else you could live with?"

Would Aunt Azar take me in? I didn't know. I didn't answer.

"Reza, come on," said Jaafer. "It'd have to be better than here."

I thought of Miles and the tar and wondered if that was true.

CHAPTER TWENTY-THREE

A few days later, Miles walked into the classroom, waving the script in the air. We all cheered.

"That was brilliant," I said when the din died down. "The old man was going to sit on this for weeks."

"That was great, Miles," echoed Jaafer. "You really got him in a corner."

"Now, now, boys," said Miles, waving for us to sit down. "You don't know. He might have approved the script sooner rather than later. But I suspect sooner might have been a month or two." A grin erupted on his ruddy face. "It *was* rather brilliant, wasn't it?"

He pulled out a calendar from his briefcase. "All right then, now we have to get busy. We need to decide on a performance date and divide up duties."

We worked on the play every minute we could. Back home we would have said this project was lame, but here we gave it everything we had.

I recruited two other boys who'd played music since they were young. I envied them for growing up in families that allowed this.

Miles found a wooden flute and lent us his old guitar. If we weren't in lockdown, we practiced. Salar became the director. They only gave us blunt tools. I guess they were afraid we'd try to make weapons out of straight pins. Omid built a small stage and a couple of boys put together costumes.

"Excellent work, Reza," Miles said one day when we sat down with the sheet music in front of us. He had come in before class for the second time that week just to work with me. "I've taught other kids, and nobody remembers so much after the first session."

"Once you show me, I hear the notes in my head. I kind of remember learning to read and this is a hundred times easier." I picked up the tar and strummed it.

"It is easier for you, but it's not for everyone." His laugh was deep and warm and made me think of a wood fire. "My sister could never get it. Lovely singing voice, but she can't transfer the notes to her head. I forget, did you tell me you don't sing?"

"When I was a kid, my dad and my uncle sang songs to me. But since the revolution it's been harder. When no one was home I would sometimes sing to myself, but I always had to be careful because Mother would get so angry."

He shook his head. "I've already flown off the handle once about this, so I'll try to stay calm. It's just so frustrating. Look how well you're doing! You're learning to read music and playing like a pro. Just think what it could have been like if you'd been playing all your life."

"I know. I've thought about that," I said quietly.

"I'll say it's been a pleasure to teach you. Really special."

I dipped my head. "Thanks."

"Have you thought about doing anything with this talent, Reza? I mean as a profession?"

"The way it looks, I'll be spending the rest of my life right here. And even if I could get home, there isn't a place for the kind of music I like."

"Not now, not today, but someday there might be. This regime won't last forever. And maybe . . ." Miles hesitated, weighing his words. "Well, never mind, I shouldn't say."

"What?" I looked up.

"I was thinking . . . just wondering . . . well, there are other places you could live, when you're older, I mean." He took the tar, checked the strings, and put it in its case. "And you'll get out of here. I still have hope. I admit it looks bleak right now, but they can't keep you here forever."

I sat, not moving. I could picture myself at home, miserable and alone. I could picture myself here. But I didn't know how to picture myself anywhere else. There was nowhere else I knew.

Miles watched me. He broke the silence. "It was just a thought, lad. Just something to mull over. Now come on, we better get to class."

✳ ✳ ✳

Working on the play was the thing that warmed us as the icy wind blew in eddies around the yard. I imagined our play going on tour and how we'd arrive at Ebi's camp. I thought about this all the time, even though I knew we didn't have per-mission to go to other camps. I'd asked Miles about it as soon as we got approval for the script, and he said, "One thing at a time." So I knew it might not happen, but I couldn't stop think-ing about it. To hear Ebi call me "Maggot" again would be like every birthday present I'd ever had rolled into one.

Other than the play, it was the same thing every day. A couple of times I helped Majid and a few boys take the garbage and load it onto a waiting truck. Or we just watched Abass herd groups of new boys from the office, their jackets still bright yellow.

Then there was the day a new boy came in—he looked so young. He had burns on one side of his face and on his arms. As I watched, the kid stumbled and whimpered. It was barely a whisper, but Abass turned on him and yelled, "What's your problem, you little Persian cockroach?" Then he hit the side of the boy's head with his big fist. The boy fell to his knees, staring at the huge guard. Tears rolled down his face.

Without thinking, I was by his side. "Leave the kid alone. Can't you tell he's terrified?"

I could feel trouble coming, like a summer storm, but something in the kid's tears made me move in front of him to face the hate in Abass's face.

Abass pointed at Salar, who'd come up behind me. "You. Take these new prisoners into the cafeteria. I'll deal with this one."

Salar, reaching for my arm, said, "Here, why don't I get Reza out of here. He's such a—"

"Go," barked Abass as he grabbed my arm and yanked me across the yard. It was all I could do to stay upright as he dragged me around the back of the classroom building, where I'd never been.

The ground was scattered with old pipes and rotting boxes. No one could see us back here, or even hear us if they'd gone in for lunch.

"I've had enough of you." Abass's voice was quiet but came from a dark place deep in his throat. "You will learn to respect those who put a roof over your head."

The smell of rust and something recently dead made me gag.

"Get ready to apologize, you insect."

I bit my lip to keep from saying the words he wanted to hear.

He stood before me, breathing hard. He slapped me fast across the face and shoved so I landed square on my butt. I struggled to get up, but my foot had wedged between two pipes and I could only push myself up on my elbows.

Abass loomed over me. For a split second I wished I could pass out to escape his rancid breath. With a painful, viselike grip, he lifted me almost to standing, yanking my foot free, and growled, "You have no idea how good you have it here. You should be grateful."

He slammed me back down on the rusty pipes and sent a swift kick to my ribs. A squeak of pain escaped, but I clamped my mouth shut to keep back a full-fledged cry.

"That didn't sound like an apology to me, ingrate." He grabbed my right hand. "Maybe if a few of your fingers just happened to break. Maybe badly enough to take you away from your precious little play." His voice got louder. "You think I won't do it?"

My stomach dropped. I knew he'd do it. He could keep me from playing and take away the only thing I knew as home.

"See if this teaches you gratitude." Abass jerked my finger away from my hand. "I'll break this finger today and save the others for later."

With a strength I didn't know I had, I wrenched my hand out of his grasp. Before Abass could touch me again, I blurted out, "I'm sorry!"

In my mind it wasn't an apology. It was a war cry. I was sorry, but I was sorry for what had happened to me, what had happened to Ebi, what had happened to all the boys growing up in this hole. I looked Abass in the face and thought about every time I'd wanted to stand up for myself and didn't. I thought about every time I'd let Mother dictate my path, and I said it again. "Yes, I am very, very sorry."

Abass dropped my hand, kicked me one more time, and left me sitting on the old pipes, trying to find my breath. I knew I should be grateful he didn't do any permanent damage, but the sound of my voice saying "sorry" echoed in my brain and I was angry—white-hot angry. When I heard boys in the yard, I realized I'd missed lunch and my friends would be looking for me. I touched my face. There would probably be a bruise where he'd hit me.

When I walked into the yard, the other boys immediately gathered around. Even little Farhad reached out to touch my arm and asked, "What happened, Rez? We were worried when Abass dragged you off."

Jaafer leaned in closer. "Looks like he took a swing."

"It could've been worse. He was planning to break my fingers if I didn't apologize, so I apologized. I need these." I smiled and flexed my still-whole fingers.

✻ ✻ ✻

Miles asked about the bruise in class the next day. I told him it was nothing, but Salar told him what had happened.

"That mongrel." He slammed his hand onto the nearest desk. "I'd like to boil his head in hot oil. I'm going to give my friends in Baghdad a call. I'll . . . I don't know what—"

"Miles, don't," I said in a quiet voice. "I'm okay. Remember what you said about not getting yourself sent home? Especially since we're so close to finishing the play. Without you we'd never get to perform it, especially not at other camps."

"All right, I hear you. I'll try to take the high road, but the man is evil." Miles wagged a finger. "And don't get your hopes up about other camps. I never promised that."

"It's possible, isn't it?" I asked.

"Let's get through our performance here, eh? We'll see what kind of drama critic our major is."

CHAPTER TWENTY-FOUR

I was careful to stay as far away from Abass as I could. We focused
on the play, filling the idle hours with talk of going home.

A few days before the first scheduled performance, the stage
was set up at the front of the vocational training room. Miles
sat in the back, grading papers while we rehearsed. I looked up
to see the major walk by with another man. After a few seconds
they were back; the major's face was pale.

"Attention," he said in his most official voice. "Stand for
General Kadrat. The general has joined us from Baghdad."

"What is going on here?" the general asked.

"As I was trying to explain," said the major, "the boys are putting on a play, a fable. . . ."

"You've seen the script?" the general asked, twirling the end of a large handlebar mustache. I was a little surprised he was speaking Farsi even though he was just talking to the major. It seemed like he wanted us to know what was happening.

"Why, yes, yes, I have, sir. Entirely harmless, I assure you. Fairly clever, actually. They speak in Farsi and Arabic." He smiled weakly. "Something for everyone."

"And why was the script not sent to me for approval?" He pulled his mustache on the other side. Miles walked to the stage.

"I . . . I didn't want to bother you with such petty details, sir." The major wiped his palms down the sides of his crisp uniform pants. "But you can certainly see it whenever you like."

"All right, I'd like a break. Let's watch it now." The general pulled a chair from behind a desk and sat down, waving his arm toward the stage. "Begin."

"You . . . you want them to do it now, sir? But we have places we need to—" stammered the major.

"That can wait." The general motioned for the major to take a seat next to him. "Begin."

We looked at each other, then at Miles. Miles looked from the stage to the general and back again twice. It was as if we were all watching a quick-moving tennis game. Then Miles clapped his hands.

"All right, men. All right. Let the show begin."

Miles's words turned on a switch. We took our places and began. At first we were stiff, nervous about this unexpected performance. But we soon relaxed into the rhythm of the work we'd practiced for so long.

I watched the audience of three when I wasn't playing. Miles beamed, his eyes sparkling with pride. The major kept stealing glances at the general.

As we began, the general stared, stone-faced, but at the first of Salar's clever puns, I saw a hint of a smile on the man's lips. When Omid popped out from behind the curtain as the angry genie, the general actually laughed. As we took our final bows, all three men clapped.

The applause made me light-headed and happy.

We shook hands and slapped one another on the back until we remembered we were in the presence of a general. We fell silent. A grave expression returned to the general's face.

"I enjoyed that performance." The general stroked his chin. "You've created something of quality with limited resources.

However, though it is well conceived and well produced, I cannot allow this performance to go on."

We gasped—all of us at the same time.

The general turned to the major. "First, it was not approved using the correct procedure. I must be informed of all activities that take place in the camps. But more importantly, it will offend those prisoners opposed to nonreligious theater. I can't have undue tension among the prisoner ranks."

Miles sprang up from his seat. His red hair seemed too bright in the room.

"But, sir, they've worked so hard for this. These are boys, most of them children when they left home. Creating this play has given them a reason to get up in the morning."

"I've made my decision. There will be no more discussion."

Miles threw up his hands in exasperation. "Do you understand the conditions these boys live under? The cruelty they endure from some of your guards? To take away this ray of hope is simply not fair. Is there no—? "

The general sounded menacing. "Sir, do not forget, you are here at my behest and I can remove you tomorrow."

Miles looked at us and took a step back.

"Major," the general said as he stood, "send these boys back to their room until lunch. I'll meet you in the office in ten minutes." To us, he said, "Thank you for the performance."

I looked over my shoulder as we walked from the room. Miles was sitting on the stage, his head in his hands. All I wanted was to sit down next to him and pretend the play had never happened.

* * *

All afternoon the songs from the play were stuck in my head. Before breakfast the next morning, Jaafer and I detoured to look into the classroom. The stage was gone. The lights were down. The props and costumes had disappeared. We looked at each other and walked on without a word. Yesterday we had played a part. We made people laugh. Today we were prisoners again.

Soon everyone in camp knew the play had been canceled. Defeat settled in our bones like the cold—a constant reminder that there was no happiness here.

Without the play to distract us, the possibility of going home was now the group obsession again. We grilled every new boy for news and begged Miles to call his Red Crescent friends. Still, at the end of every week, all we had were rumors and gossip.

One freezing morning, the major summoned us into the yard. He stood against the wall with a megaphone in his hand. The sun was barely up. The sky above the yard was filled with dark gray clouds shaped like leopard spots, turning pink in the growing light.

"What's this about? What's going on?" echoed from each clump of boys as we gathered.

"Not a clue."

There was chatter about going home.

"Is this it?"

"Will they take us all?"

"Maybe just the younger ones and they'll leave the rest of us to rot."

Excitement spread from face to face. What if they made deals for going home camp by camp? What if I went home and Ebi was left in the northern camp?

The major brought the megaphone to his lips and spoke in his heavy accent. "Gentlemen, I know you've all been talking about the Red Crescent's efforts to negotiate your release."

A ripple of murmurs moved through us.

"But you need to hear this from your own leader. There is a pertinent message that came from your Ayatollah Khomeini." He read from a piece of paper that fluttered in the wind: *"They are not Iranian children. Ours have gone to paradise and we shall see them there."*

The major continued, "Although we will keep a dialogue open, you must understand that this strong statement ends any current hopes of sending you home." The major folded his arms over his chest, as if watching for a reaction.

At first there was no sound at all. The major's words—*our* leader's words—had sucked the breath from all of us. Then several boys fell to their knees with their heads in their hands. A whisper spread from one boy to the next; confusion turned to anger.

Jaafer and Omid joined the boys who waved their fists, yelling. Farhad leaned into his crutches, tears streaming down his face. Pasha knelt on the ground, pounding the dust. Salar had no expression on his face at all, which scared me more than anything.

The major spoke again—words upon words—but no one was listening. All we heard were our private thoughts of home, the home we would probably never see again.

CHAPTER TWENTY-FIVE

Weeks passed. Farhad and Pasha were among the few boys who knelt when the call to prayer sounded. Sometimes we talked about trying to escape, but the conversation always died before it really began.

Somewhere there must have been signs of spring. Green buds. The scent of flowers. But not here. Here was sand and beige and always more sand.

One morning Salar gestured to the never-ending football game. "Gentlemen, care to join us in this game?"

I shook my head. "There's going to be a canyon where these guys run back and forth, back and forth across this yard. Maybe if I ever see a real pitch again, I'll want to play, but right now I'm just so tired of it all."

"I only asked out of habit," said Salar. "I feel the same way. It would be really nice if we could do something else."

Miles walked up behind us. " 'Morning, boys. I'd say *lovely morning*, but it's not really, is it? It's dusty and hot, and by afternoon this shirt will be stuck to my back. Stinks, eh?"

We nodded and gave Miles the courtesy of a chuckle. A jeep pulled in and Salar said, "Hey, Reza, here comes the next load of boys. Fish Butt is scarce, but I'm still thinking you might want to stay away from them, huh?"

I looked in the direction of the office, then turned away. "Absolutely. I don't even want to look at them. Miles, can we go to the classroom? Maybe we can sneak in a game of cards."

"We can," said Miles, but he hesitated.

Suddenly I heard running footsteps behind me. I wheeled around and almost fell over. There, coming toward me, was Ebi! Or was it? Could this really be him? An ugly scar ran down the side of his face. When I saw his left arm was missing below the elbow, my heart lurched. But yes, it was Ebi!

I yelled his name. Then, part yelling, part sobbing, I said, "How? What? I can't believe you're here."

"I'm here, Maggot," Ebi replied in a voice smaller than I remembered. "I can't believe it, either."

I didn't know what to do. I grabbed my old friend and held on to him like a lifeline. Ebi whispered, "I thought I was going to die so many times. I thought I'd never see you again, Rez."

Tears ran down my cheeks and I choked on my words, "But you're here, man. I can't believe you're here."

We stood holding on to each other's shoulders for what seemed like forever. We took turns starting to talk and being too choked up and then laughing until we finally both stopped crying.

I saw Miles smiling over Ebi's shoulder.

"Miles, did you know about this?" Remembering Salar and Jaafer were there, I turned to them. "Salar, Jaafer, this is Ebi. Miles, did you have anything to do with this? Why didn't you tell me?"

"I put the wheels in motion, lad, but I didn't know if it would work. Didn't want to tell you because it was a long shot. I asked Majid to bunk him with you, too, so if he worked that out, you guys better behave."

I nodded slowly. "Thanks." I wanted to say more but couldn't think of any words that were good enough.

"They told me I was coming here this morning," said Ebi, softly. "But I just wasn't going to believe it until I got here." He shook his head. "You look good. You look older."

"We're so much older, right?" I put an arm around Ebi, smiled, and said, "Salar, mind if I steal your job? Mind if I get this one acclimated?"

Salar gave a huge flourish of his arm and said, "Be my guest."

Once Ebi and the others in his group had their yellow canvas pants, we took them to the classroom. Word spread that Ebi was there, and one by one my other friends arrived.

"You're the famous Ebi?" asked Omid. "I thought you'd be wearing a cape and have superpowers, the way the chump here described you."

Ebi laughed but didn't have a quick comeback like I would have expected. Everybody went around the room making introductions. I kept grinning at Ebi, then grinning at Miles. I felt like a kite, soaring, playing tag with the wind. Life in camp was no better than before Ebi had come, but at least for today I didn't have to think about that.

Either Majid had worked his magic or it was an awesome coincidence, because Ebi and another kid from the morning's crew of new boys were placed in our room for lockdown. Ebi and I moved to the back, and the other boys left us alone. For a few minutes we were quiet. It was as if we didn't know where to start.

Finally I said, "I was in the hospital for almost two months." I pointed to Ebi's arm. "It must have been worse for you."

"About three months."

"Does it still hurt?"

Ebi rubbed the stump of his arm. "Doesn't hurt much now. But it's weird. Sometimes I feel my hand. I swear it's there, but when I look down, of course it's not."

"Man," I whispered. "I'm sorry."

Ebi looked straight into my eyes. "No, Rez. I'm the one who's sorry. You wouldn't be here if it wasn't for me."

"It would've happened anyway. My mother would have pressured me to go sooner or later."

"But maybe you wouldn't have been caught in that mine-field."

"Ebi, haven't you heard? Everyone was sent to the fields— pretty much every single one of us in all these camps. That's the strategy. We die better than we fight. We aren't old enough to handle those big guns. But we're big enough to set off a mine. Clear the way for the older troops to come through."

We both stared into space. I thought about our last morning

together. It'd been less than a year ago, but it seemed like a lifetime.

"What was your camp like?" I asked. "Was it as bad as they say?"

"It's bad. Someone disappears every week, and the rest of us were beat up all the time." Ebi fingered the collar of his shirt nervously. "I got beat pretty bad the day the guys from here were transferred in and I found out you were alive. Guess I went a little wild. Later I couldn't sleep 'cause everything hurt, but it was okay. I lay awake for hours, wondering if I'd ever see you again. Wondering if I'd ever see my parents." He smiled at me. "But I'm here. Maybe that means I might see my folks again, too."

"Miles thinks it'll happen someday. Not soon, but he thinks it will." I worked at a piece of loose linoleum on the floor. "I don't think I can go home. My mother wouldn't want me there."

Ebi didn't argue. "You can come live with us. My sister wouldn't have a chance against the two of us." In a flash, I saw my old friend in the face across from me. But it passed, leaving only the sad pools that were now Ebi's eyes.

"Tell me about Miles," he said. "There's nobody like him at Camp Twelve."

"I'm not sure there's anyone like him anywhere." I grinned.

"He's taught me to read music, and he has a tar that he lets me play. Makes life bearable to have him here."

"Well, I don't know what he did, but if it helped get me out of that camp, he probably saved my life."

I looked at my friend and nodded slowly. "I think he saved mine, too."

CHAPTER TWENTY-SIX

The next day, I hung back so I could say something to Miles. Ebi went with Salar to lunch. As I walked toward the desk, Miles put his pen down and chuckled. "Can't believe we actually got him here."

"I don't know what to say, Miles. I don't know how to thank you." I shook my head slowly. "I'm so grateful, but I'm not sure I understand why you did it."

He laughed. "I might say 'because I could,' and that's part of it. But I don't know that I've ever seen anyone care for a friend the way you care for Ebi. You weren't going to let that friendship go, and for someone like you, someone who's seen so much—well, that was impressive. When I saw I could honor that, it just made sense."

I could feel myself blushing. "I guess I'll just say thanks again and hope you know what it really means."

Miles stood up and gave my shoulder a squeeze. "I've got it. Now get to lunch. You'll want to teach Ebi about staying away from Pasha and Abass."

Ebi slipped into the fabric of my friends, and every day was a little less awful because he was there. Still, right away I realized things were different. All our lives Ebi had set the pace: where we went and what we did. Now, even though we didn't have much choice, he looked to me to decide. Before the war Ebi would have jousted with Salar or Jaafer for their place as clown. I waited for Ebi to step up to his customary place as he settled in, but as the weeks went by, the one-armed Ebi was happy to sit in the second row.

One Monday morning a few weeks after Ebi's arrival, Miles was late for class. Sometimes we'd had to wait a minute or two for him, but fifteen minutes went by with no word.

"This is very strange," said Omid. "He was here last Friday, right? And he was supposed to be here today."

"Yeah, he taught that French class in the morning," said

Salar. "Then I saw him rescue one of those new little kids when two guards started pushing the kid around."

Fear skimmed my brain. A minute later when Miles walked through the door, my fists relaxed on the desk in front of me. But they balled up again when I saw the two bright spots of color on Miles's white face. Something was wrong.

Jaafer glanced at me and I looked at Omid. But nobody said anything until Miles sat down at his desk and slowly unpacked his case. Finally Salar couldn't wait. "Miles, what happened? What's wrong?"

Miles looked up. He seemed to take us all in for the first time. "I've been sacked, boys. They kicked me out."

Before he'd finished his last sentence I felt like I was going to throw up. Even the boys who weren't as close to Miles gasped, looking for their next breath.

I was the first to say something. "No, Miles. Why? They can't do that!"

Miles caught my eyes and held them. When he spoke he sounded old and tired. "I'm afraid they can. I don't know exactly why, but the major was very clear. I've overstayed my welcome and they control my visa. I have a day to settle things here, then I'm on a Red Crescent plane that leaves Baghdad on Friday."

"Friday," wailed Salar. "Why Friday? If you had more time

maybe you could get your journalist buddies to change his mind."

"Believe me, I've been arguing this for hours." Miles stared out the high window as if he could see something we couldn't. "I'm afraid there isn't anything else to do. Don't worry, I'll make sure they get someone else in here soon. Someone a bit less volatile than this Irish lunatic, eh, lads?"

We all started to talk at once. My head pounded, and I felt sweat on the back of my neck. Through the noise Miles clapped his hands, making me jump. "All right, boys. That's enough. For now we are going to forget this and have a normal class. I'll come in again tomorrow or the next day for good-byes."

I don't remember the rest of class. I don't remember lunch or how I got back to lockdown. It was almost as if Uncle had died again. I lay on my mat, oblivious to the talk around me. I told myself it wasn't the same as losing Uncle. Miles was alive and well. Miles was going away, but sometime, somewhere, I might see him again. But what it felt like was that Father was dead and Uncle was dead and Miles was leaving. It felt like loving people made no sense.

The next morning I woke up wanting to talk to Miles. I hadn't really talked to him the day before. I'd been too dazed, but today I wondered if we could figure out a way for him to stay. I'd push him again to call his friends at the Red Crescent to see if they could make a case for him. Maybe the major was in a better mood today and could be reasoned with.

From the yard I watched for the opportunity to slip away. I edged toward the classroom building and after a while saw my chance to slide through the door. Just outside the classroom, I heard Miles and Salar talking. I crept closer and listened.

"I told you boys the truth, Salar." Miles's voice was quiet but clear. "I'm not sure why they've ousted me. But I asked you to come here because I have a nagging fear it might be because Abass has developed an obsessive hatred for a few of you boys, and he's done with me interfering. You remember I stepped in to rescue Reza a while back. Then two weeks ago I stepped in while he was beating on a boy barely twelve. This little kid may have been the last straw."

"It's not fair."

"No, it's not fair. Not fair at all. But it is what it is. I want to ask you to keep watch. I don't want you to step in. You're not one of Abass's favorites, yourself. Just try to keep the boys away from him. Especially Reza. I might not have done him any favors when I interfered that time."

"I will."

Miles let out a low laugh. "Sorry I'm asking you to be the grown-up, Salar. It's just until we can get someone else in here who can best you and Omid, eh?"

I could barely hear Salar's answer. "Yeah, right . . . right . . . sure."

"Come on, boy. Give this old Irish idiot a hug. Then I'll ask you to go fetch Reza. I'd like to have a word with him before the big good-bye session."

I turned, tiptoed down the hall, and went back into the sunlight. Salar was distracted. It took him a few minutes to find me even though I was in plain sight, watching him.

"Miles is in the classroom. Wants to see you."

"No new news?" I asked. "I mean, he's still planning to leave?"

"Looks that way."

"I can't believe it," I said, trying to keep from choking up.

"You can say that twice," Salar said as he walked off in the other direction.

I said it again under my breath as I headed to the classroom.

"Reza, come on in. Thanks for coming by."

"Miles, do you—"

Miles held his hand up. "Stop, before you go on. I *do* have to leave. They've kicked me out. It's dangerous for you boys and for me if I stay. If I go now I should be able to get a decent replacement. If I fight any longer to stay, they may decide it's not worth it to teach you boys at all." He sat down on the desk and waved me to a chair next to him.

"A few things I want to say, lad. First and most important is to make you understand how critical it is for you to keep your head down and stay out of trouble. Abass isn't a schoolyard bully. He's a dangerous man, and there is no question the authorities here will take his side over yours. No question."

Miles reached out and tilted my head up to look at him. "It would mean a lot to me if you promised to stay out of his way."

"I will, Miles." My mouth was dry, and the walls of the room felt like they'd moved six feet closer.

"Good. Next I want you to know that I'm leaving you the tar. They won't let you keep it in lockdown, of course, but I'll leave it with Majid. He can make sure that when they let you boys out of here, you can take this baby with you." He patted the leather case that lay on the desk behind him. "Maybe he can entrust it to the learned scholar who comes to take my place and you won't have to wait too long to play it again."

"Thank you, Mil—" but the rest of the word stuck in my throat.

Miles pulled a chair up next to me. The sound of the scraping reminded me of the day I dove through the window to reach the tar. It felt like yesterday and it felt like my childhood.

"The last thing is—I want to give you this." Miles handed me a small folded piece of paper. I held it without opening it. "That's my mum's address. You can always reach me through her. Someday you will get out of here. Someday things will calm down in this part of the world. And on that someday, I want you to get on a plane and come visit your old friend Miles."

"I've never been on a plane," I whispered.

"Well, all the more reason to come." Miles took a deep breath. "Reza, it's not my place to tell you what to believe or what kind of man you're going to be. Not my place." He lifted my face again to meet his eyes. He held it there between his big hands. "But, Reza, you are special, a unique soul. You need to see enough of the world so you can choose who you'll grow up to be. I'd be honored, I'd be truly privileged, if you'd let me be a guide for some of that journey."

I didn't trust myself to speak so I nodded. Miles stood, extended his hand and pulled me up. I reached my arms and hugged him as tightly as I could, and he rested his chin lightly on my head. "Just come find me, lad," he said hoarsely. "Just come find me."

I nodded again and found my voice at last. "I will, Miles. I promise, I will."

CHAPTER TWENTY-SEVEN

The next morning I saw what I was thinking reflected on other faces. Miles was gone. This day, the next, and every day we could imagine was going to be the same. Empty and colorless. So much dust swirled around the yard, I could barely see the other side. Ebi, Jaafer, and I sat with our backs against the wall. We kept our heads down and our mouths closed to lock out the dirt.

When the bell rang for lunch, we rushed in to get out of the grime. Everyone had the same thought. In an instant a crowd of boys gathered at the door to the cafeteria. I waited for the line in front of me to move, trying not to smell the onions I'd eaten every day for almost a year.

Without warning, the boy behind me stumbled, pushing me into the crowd. I fell, landing full force against someone's feet. My heart sank when I heard Pasha's voice.

"Just what I'd expect. Reza the Ingrate trying to start trouble."

I stood up quickly. "Pasha, it was an accident. I got pushed. I didn't mean—"

"Don't make excuses, moron." Pasha shoved my shoulder hard enough that I fell back. The stench of sweat and boys surrounded me.

I took an angry step toward Pasha, my blood boiling, my fists clenched. Then, like another hit, I remembered my promise to Miles to stay out of trouble. I stepped back, raised my hands in surrender, and said, "Okay, Pasha, I'm sorry. I'll be more careful next time."

Pasha stood and glared. I turned to Ebi. "Let's get out of here. We'll go to the back of the line."

I felt my collar tighten as someone grabbed it from behind. I twisted to see Abass standing over me.

"I suspected I'd find you in the middle of a brawl."

"It's not a brawl, sir," I said, struggling to be polite. "Someone tripped and knocked me into the crowd. No problems here."

"No problems—that's right, because I'm going to remove you from any temptation." Abass gripped my arm and dragged me away. "See how you like being by yourself for a while."

Several boys spoke, trying to defend me, but Abass silenced them with a swing of his club in their direction. The last thing I saw as the guard spun me around was Pasha's grinning face.

Abass led me down a dark hall and into a small room barely big enough to turn around in. It smelled like it had been closed for months, and the last time it was used was as a latrine. I started to curse but held my tongue, seeing Miles's face, hearing my promise.

Abass stood in the open doorway. He reached for his belt and pulled his knife from its sheath. The blade caught the light from the hall. Before I knew what was happening, Abass slapped me hard and I went down, my hands and knees connecting with the concrete floor at the same time. Almost immediately, his steel-toed boot hit my ribs. His second kick landed in the same place he'd kicked me weeks before. It was still tender and I rolled away from him, trying to protect myself, but the room was so small I had nowhere to go. He pushed me into the corner. With one huge hand he held me in place;

with the other he punched my stomach. I groaned. He laughed and punched me again.

"I got some lip for those bruises I gave you before, but none of these are going to show." He pushed me harder against the wall. "And you aren't going to talk about our time together— understand? If you do I'll finish you and come after your little friend." He brought his knee up hard between my legs. I couldn't breathe, and what little light there was in the room went all sparkly. I'm not sure what happened next. I was only half-conscious on the floor while he kicked me again and again, rhythmically chanting something in Arabic. I couldn't really hear him through the pounding in my ears. At some point he stopped and pulled me up, bringing his huge forearm across my chest, his knife at my throat.

"Feel this, idiot?" The tip of the blade pressed cold against my skin.

"Yes," I whispered. Of course I did. I felt everything and everything hurt.

"I am going to cut you now, but just a little." My legs shook. I felt a prick and a sharp jab just under my Adam's apple. Abass released me. "I don't want you to die just yet."

He turned and left, snickering as he locked the door and left me in darkness. I moved slowly, feeling my ribs. I didn't think anything was broken, but I was going to hurt for days. My hand went to my neck. There was blood, but I knew it wasn't as bad as it could have been. Abass was good with the knife. He could toy with me for months or kill me in an instant.

I sat, my hand on my neck, trying to breathe normally, waiting for my eyes to adjust. As the minutes ticked by I still couldn't see my outstretched hand. When the bleeding on my neck stopped I felt my way around the small room, avoiding the floor for fear of finding what I smelled. My hands found a rough canvas cot; I brushed it off with my sleeve and sank down.

Every time the fear of Abass gripped my stomach, I tried to think of something else. I thought about what it would be like to take Miles up on his offer. I realized I didn't know if he was going to his mother's in Belfast or someplace else. Could I live with him? What kind of music would there be?

I heard the distant sounds of the boys going to afternoon lockdown. I tried to remember every song I knew and sang softly to myself. Hours later I heard the boys heading to dinner. I longed for another helping of the gruel I'd had for breakfast what seemed a lifetime ago.

The sounds of the camp drifted away into occasional footsteps in the distance. I wondered if Abass would leave me here until I starved.

I finally drifted into sleep. A few minutes or a few hours later, I heard the lock turn. I stood up, wincing but awake and alert. I was not going to face Abass lying down. The light of a flashlight blinded me. Before I could see, I heard a lyrical voice I didn't recognize. "Reza, are you here? Are you all right?"

I squinted. It was Majid. I'd never thought about it before, but just then I realized that we'd hardly ever spoken, just a word here or there.

"I'm okay," I croaked.

"What did he do to you?" Majid shone the flashlight up and down my body. "Can you walk?"

I straightened and tried to move normally. "It's not bad, but how did you know? And what are you doing here? Abass will kill you if he finds you."

"He won't find me here. We both went off duty hours ago." Majid led me by flashlight as he spoke. "Five of us went for dinner at Barsam's house, and Abass drank a lot of whiskey."

"Abass? Drank whiskey? I thought he was religious."

"He puts on that show, but away from the camp, away from his family, it is different." Majid opened a door that led to the deserted kitchen. He steered me to the sink, wet a cloth, and placed it on my neck, swearing under his breath. "I am not cut out for this job. Most of the others turn away when Abass and his kind torture you boys. I think some even like it. But I can't stand it." He shook his head.

"Majid, it's okay. I'm fine."

"He spent the first two drinks laughing about how he'd beaten you and locked you up and the last three talking about his plan to torture and kill you."

I took a deep breath, remembering Miles's words for the hundredth time. "Majid, maybe it's not safe for you to help me."

"Most everyone on duty now is asleep. You'll be back in your room in a few minutes. Abass is passed out at Barsam's house and doesn't go on duty until tomorrow afternoon. He'll never know who let you out."

Majid crossed to a huge refrigerator and brought out a pot, placed it on the range, and lit the fire. After stirring a few times he turned to face me.

"My young friend, you need to be very careful. I've seen Abass when he gets like this. He has killed before. He could kill you. You must make it your job to give him no reason to touch you."

"I try, but he looks for reasons to come down on me."

Majid nodded. "I never understand why he takes such a disliking to some boys. Your friendship with Mr. Miles didn't help matters. Abass did not like Mr. Miles." His brow furrowed, he filled a bowl with hot soup from the pot and placed it in front of me.

The soup smelled delicious. I ate a spoonful and nearly yelled with surprise. "Majid, there's meat in this soup—and vegetables, too!"

Majid smiled and nodded. "It's from the major's lunch yesterday, I assume." He motioned to the refrigerator. "I took it from his shelf." He ran his hand across his forehead, the momentary smile gone. "With Mr. Miles gone and Abass in this state, you are very vulnerable. You must be careful."

"I'll try to blend in, stay out of his sight." The hot soup made me feel for a fleeting second that this might actually be possible.

CHAPTER TWENTY-EIGHT

Majid let me into our room. All the boys were sleeping. I slipped off my shoes and shuffled to my mat at the far end of the room. I lay down and pulled up the thin blanket.

"What happened? Are you all right?" Ebi asked so quietly I wasn't sure I'd heard.

"Sorry, did I wake you?"

"I wasn't sleeping. Until a while ago we were all up, worried about you, wondering where you were." Ebi turned on his side to face me. "Did he hurt you again?"

My hand went to my neck. "Mostly he tried to scare me." I stared at the ceiling for a minute without saying anything. "I guess he did scare me."

On my other side Jaafer mumbled something in his sleep and rolled over. I turned to face Ebi so I could whisper and not be heard.

"Ebi, I think we need to get out of here. I think Abass is crazy—at least when he's around me—and I think he might really kill me. Remember the small guard I pointed out the other day, Majid? He's the one who let me out. He says Abass has killed before. He's worried. We need to go—soon."

"Rez, what are you thinking? There's no way out of here."

"I've been thinking about it." I put my mouth close to Ebi's ear. "I don't know if you've noticed yet, but Majid is usually responsible for taking the garbage out, and we sometimes help him. We could get Omid or Salar to do something to distract the guards in the yard. Then we could hide in the truck and jump off as far from here as we can. It'd be the next meal before they knew we were missing."

"Then what?"

"I don't know. We find our way to Baghdad."

I could just make out Ebi glaring at me in the gloom. "I don't know, Rez. What would happen in Baghdad? We don't really speak the language. We can't get jobs. We might not ever make it home."

"Come on. We can go to the Red Crescent office. If we get out tomorrow, we might be in time to see Miles, and he can set us up with someone."

Ebi's eyes widened. "You're thinking of going with Miles, aren't you?"

"No," I said quickly, but the minute he said it, I realized I had been thinking just that. "Come on, Ebi. It'll finally be the adventure you wanted."

Ebi looked back at me, and in the dim glow that came from the outside lights, I could see tears in my friend's eyes.

"I just got here, Rez. It's a better place than where I came from. I just want to stay here until I go home. We'll keep you away from Abass. If we stay with you all the time, he can't get to you."

I felt a spark of rage. My old friend Ebi would have been pulling me out the door. But war had taken my old friend and left me this shell. Still, shell or not, I wasn't leaving without him.

"All right. But I'm holding you to that, understand?"

Ebi grabbed my arm with his only hand. "You got it, Maggot."

I rolled onto my back. I tried to sleep but everything hurt and I kept feeling the point of Abass's knife at my throat.

I must have drifted off, because I woke to my friends yelling my name.

"Reza," said Jaafer, grabbing my shoulder. "When did you get back? What happened to you?"

Omid put a finger to my neck. "Man! Did Abass do this? Are you okay?"

As we headed out I retold the story, vowing to stay far away from Abass.

When I walked into the cafeteria, I saw Abass glowering at me from across the room. Majid had said he wasn't supposed to be here until this afternoon, but here he was. I felt like I could smell him from across the room. He didn't look happy. His eyes looked bloodshot even from a distance.

We spooned the watery cereal into bowls. Abass waited less than sixty seconds before he crossed to our table. We all froze as he placed his hands on my shoulders.

"Well, well. I wonder who let you out of your fine accommodations last night. No one seems to know, but I'll find out." I winced as Abass leaned down. "I control you, boy. I control you all, but you"—he slapped me on the back of my head, hard—"I might just need to make an example of you. Remember what I told you."

He picked up my bowl and walked away.

Salar slammed a fist into his other hand. "Reza, he is scary. What's he talking about—an example?"

"Nothing. He's just trying to scare me." It was working, but if Ebi and I weren't going to make a run for it, I didn't want everyone as freaked out as I was.

"That wasn't nothing, Reza." Omid pushed his bowl away. "What did he say?"

My hand moved to my neck. I quickly placed it palm down on the table. "When he cut me, he said he wasn't ready to kill me quite yet."

"Ape," said Salar and Jaafer at the same time.

"Quiet, you guys." I wheeled around to see where Abass was. If he'd heard them, we'd all be in solitary.

"Reza, he really has it out for you, maybe because he knows Miles liked you." Omid looked over his shoulder in the direction Abass had gone. "Whatever, it's not good, chump. Maybe we should find a way to hide you. Or even better, get you out of here."

I glanced at Ebi, then shrugged. "It's okay. I need to be really careful, that's all."

"But if he's serious, we may not be able to protect you," whispered Salar. "I think Omid's right. We need to find a way to help you escape. Get you to the Red Crescent in Baghdad or something. I wish Miles was still here."

"Come on, guys. It's okay. I'll—"

Ebi spoke for the first time all morning, interrupting. "Reza has a plan. He thinks he can stow away on the garbage truck next time he helps load. Then when he's out of camp, he'll jump off and make a run for it. All it would take is for someone to cause a distraction so the guards wouldn't notice anyone missing."

I didn't like the way Ebi was talking about me stowing away; he didn't say "we" at all.

"That might just work," said Omid.

"I don't know." I looked around to make sure no one could hear. "Seems risky, and if I fail, then Abass would have reason to have my head."

Ebi looked straight at me. "Reza liked the plan last night, but he wanted me to go with him and I said no. So suddenly the plan is no good."

The boys all looked at me expectantly. I looked back at them and then down at my hands. "I waited a long time for the little cockroach to catch up with me. I'm not leaving him behind now."

Ebi let out a rusty laugh. "All right, Maggot. I'll go with you.

If you stay here because of me and get yourself killed by that bastard, there'll be no living with these guys."

Everyone talked at once. I caught Ebi's eye. I saw fear and resignation and a shard of the Ebi I thought I'd lost.

CHAPTER TWENTY-NINE

In the yard, we took a ball and went to a deserted corner. As we passed the ball back and forth at short range, we worked out every permutation of the plan. Majid arrived for his shift. He barely looked in our direction.

"Are you ready to go right away if we can make it happen?" asked Salar.

"I guess," I said. "We might lose our nerve if we wait around."

Ebi nodded.

The thought of Miles's plane drummed its fingers on the back of my brain.

"But what about you guys?" I felt stupid for not thinking of this before. "What if they find out you knew?"

"They won't find out," said Salar. "We'll tell them ever since Ebi got here, you two had been keeping secrets."

"Don't worry, chump," said Omid. "We dealt with Abass and his crew before you got here; we'll deal with him until we leave."

"But what if—"

"Shut up and stop worrying," said Farhad. I thought about how much I'd miss these guys.

Jaafer disappeared and came back a few minutes later with a piece of paper and a pencil hidden in his hand. "I wrote my address here." He passed it to Salar. "When things get back to normal, find us. We'll all meet in Tehran. We'll have a real party."

"Sounds good to me," said Salar as he wrote on the paper. "You'll buy dinner, Reza."

Minutes after Omid had scribbled down his information and handed it to me, Majid and a younger guard came out of the classroom building dragging several trash cans. My heart leaped. It was time to go.

"Do I look casual now?" I cuffed Ebi on the shoulder. "Come

on, Ebi. We'll go and nonchalantly offer to help and not let on that we're nervous as rats in a cage."

"Right behind you, Maggot."

In turn I looked at my friends—Omid, Salar, Farhad, and Jaafer, my mate from the beginning. "If this works, I'll buy you all the finest meal you could ever imagine."

"Holding you to it," said Jaafer over his shoulder as he followed the others to the far side of the yard.

Approaching Majid, I reached for a trash can. "Could you use some help, sir?"

"I suppose we could." He pointed in the direction of a large can twenty yards away. "If you boys bring that can, we will bring these." As the other guard moved off, Majid quietly said, "I notice he came in this morning. Did you steer clear as I instructed?"

"I've tried, sir, but it isn't going to be easy."

"No," Majid said, taking his cans and walking toward the gate in the back fence.

Ebi and I lifted the large can together and followed. I felt every blow Abass had landed. It took all I had not to let on. When we reached the gate, Majid had it open and was bringing the first of his cans through to a waiting truck. The truck bed was already half-filled with garbage. As we emptied the cans sitting next to the truck, my stomach churned at the thought of crouching in that slop. Ebi's face was slightly green.

We helped the other guard lift the final can and then heard the noise we'd been waiting for. Yells and screaming broke out in the yard. Both guards whipped around and headed toward the disturbance.

This was it. I hauled myself into the truck, cleared a hiding place for us, and grabbed for Ebi's hand.

Ebi took it but didn't jump up. "Look, Rez, this is going to work better if I cover for you. I'm sorry, I can't leave. Go. Stay alive and come find me at home. May God watch over you."

Ebi let go and was gone before I knew what to do. I started to get up, to follow my friend back into the camp, but Ebi, already a few paces from the truck, turned and shook his head. His lips formed the word "go," and he ran to meet up with the two guards, who were on their way back with one more can.

"What's going on?" asked Ebi, his voice a little louder than necessary.

"Looks like a fight," said the younger guard. "The other guards have it under control. Not surprising that hothead Pasha's there in the middle of it. All you need to do is say a cross word to that one and he's likely to deck you."

Majid pulled out the truck keys.

The younger guard said, "Hey, where's that other kid? The one who was helping you?"

"Didn't you see him?" asked Ebi. "He ran to the fight as soon as we heard it. He's always fighting with Pasha."

"He did?" The guard looked at the truck, where he couldn't see me behind the stinking piles, then back to the mass of yellow-suited boys on the other side of the yard. "I didn't see him go. Did you, Majid?"

Majid quickly looked at the truck and down at Ebi, then back at the truck again. I held my breath. Would he give me away?

"What?" Majid said stiffly. "Oh, yes, I saw him. He's a bit of a hothead, too, isn't he? Here, give me that last can. I'll have a talk with him when I get back from garbage duty."

I heard footsteps coming toward the truck, and the heavy tailgate slammed shut.

As Majid hoisted himself into the driver's seat, I thought maybe I could still jump out, go back to camp, go back to Ebi, and pretend . . . pretend what? Nothing. I'd made the leap and I couldn't go back. I'd found Ebi and now he was gone again. I sank back down in the muck and put my head in my hands.

The truck started up and lurched forward. I tried to hold back my tears, but as the rumble of the truck grew louder, I cried almost as if I wanted to be heard. I sat among the rotting vegetables and flies and sobbed. I thought I would cry all the way to Baghdad if Majid kept on driving, but in less than ten minutes the truck veered to the side of the road.

Majid came running to the back of the truck. He called softly, "Reza. Reza, are you there?"

Wiping my eyes with my dirty sleeve, I crept out. "I'm sorry, Majid. I—"

"No apologies. You did what you had to do, but we don't have much time. Follow me." We'd reached the outskirts of a town and had pulled up parallel to a short alley. I jumped off the truck and followed Majid toward an old brick building. "I'm guessing they'll send someone to meet me at the dump to search the truck. It must look like I came straight away with no detours. I'll hide you here and come back to get you later."

"Majid, you don't have to do this. Just don't report me and I'll find my way."

"Don't be ridiculous, boy. They'll have the word out all over the region. Boys don't escape from our camps. At least that's what they like to say."

"You mean others have escaped—"

"No time." He cut me off. "Come along now."

Majid opened a door and motioned me in. "This is my

brother's apartment building. If you stay here in the storage room, you should be safe. I'll be back for you as soon as I can. But remember—stay right here, hidden. If anyone sees you in that yellow suit—or smells you—you'll be at Abass's feet within the hour."

CHAPTER THIRTY

Majid was gone. I stood in the semidarkness, dazed. It was the first time in over a year I'd been anywhere but the hospital or the camp. I was in a room full of the things people didn't keep in their apartments. The sight of a couple of bicycles and some stacked wooden chairs cheered me in an odd way. They were so normal and so extraordinary at the same time.

I sat on the floor and tried not to think about what I'd done. Tried not to think about Ebi. I held an old newspaper up to the half light. It dated from 1976, before the revolution. Ancient history. I leaned back and closed my eyes. What was Miles doing now? What was happening with Jaafer and Ebi and the others? Even though they said they weren't worried, I was so afraid they'd be in trouble because of me.

I occupied my mind trying to remember all the songs I'd learned from Miles and Uncle. After listening to the sounds in the building, I drifted off.

Suddenly I heard voices outside. I couldn't follow the conversation—it was in Arabic—but it was right outside the door. Creeping farther into the shadows, I picked up an old pipe and held it above my head. Before too long the people talking went their separate ways, wishing each other well. It took me a few more minutes to relax enough to lower the pipe.

The places where Abass had hit me were still stiff, and I was starving. The soup Majid had given me was a distant memory, and Abass had taken my breakfast.

A kaleidoscope of emotions hit me. I had escaped but had no idea where I was or what my next move would be. Majid had said he'd be back as soon as he could, but did that mean today? Every hour that passed I thought about my friends back at the camp, willing myself not to wish I were back with them.

The hungrier I got, the harder it was to stop myself from wondering if I'd ever see any of them again. Especially Ebi. How could I have spent all those months trying to find him, just to leave him again? I made myself stand up and move, trying to shake these thoughts out of my head. I didn't leave him—he left me.

I needed food badly. Maybe I could sneak out and find some food nearby. I opened the door a millimeter, but through the slit I could see enough to know that it was not possible. I had no money, and I was wearing a bright yellow uniform that was basically a neon sign declaring ESCAPED PRISONER.

I looked back into the room. Maybe someone had some food stored here. Floor-to-ceiling shelves next to the door seemed like a good place to start. I searched methodically from shelf to shelf. I found boxes of nails, old newspapers and books, a space heater that was falling apart, and a dozen other things that were not nor had ever been food.

It took me ages to go through every shelf and box in the room. I almost gagged from the moldy smell. But just before giving up, I found a round tin that had once been full of nuts. The eight cashews still inside were stale, but I ate them anyway.

I was running my finger along the bottom of the tin when, off in the distance, I heard the call to prayer. Unlike the tinny microphone I'd heard in the camp, this sounded like home. I looked around the room in confusion. What time was it? How long had I slept? Was this the noon prayer? No, the light was slanting in from the one high window. It must be late afternoon. I took a piece of cardboard, spread it on the dirt floor, and knelt down to pray.

I fell into the familiar chant like it was my old bed at home—somewhere I felt warm and comfortable. Somewhere I could rest. Somewhere I could be in this moment and put that heavy box labeled UNKNOWN FUTURE aside for a minute. After prayers were over I sat in that calm and watched the room grow dark. I tried not to think. By the next call to prayer the room was almost completely dark. A glimmer from a flickering streetlight let me see shapes around me but nothing more.

As the last *Come to prayer! Come to prayer!* drifted through the town, I knelt on the cardboard and fell into the rhythm again. When I was finished I lay on my side, adjusted my bruised ribs away from the hard floor, and was asleep before I curled my arms under my head.

Sometime later a truck clattered by on the street outside. I stood up before I was really awake. It was freezing. Every muscle was stiff; every injury was sore. The calm from my prayers had faded. I paced. I opened the door a crack. I paced some more and then took a few steps outside. I wondered whether I should leave now, while it was dark and the streets were empty. I might have a better chance of finding some other clothes. I went a little farther into the street. I looked left and right. Then I heard another truck around the corner and had just enough time to jump back into my hideout.

My heart beat like a bass drum during a long solo. I stood stock-still and listened while another truck went by. I realized it must be early morning and I'd missed any chance I might have had to leave. What if something had happened to Majid? Maybe he was in trouble for helping me. Maybe they were all in trouble because of my stupid scheme, and here I was, no closer to being safe than when Abass beat me.

Just then I heard footsteps, and the door started to open. I scooted back into a dark corner and made myself as small as possible. I looked around for the pipe, but it was across the room where I'd left it last night. I don't know what I thought I'd do with it anyway. I pulled back farther into the corner. A man in work pants and a jacket grabbed an old bike and started out the door. I held my breath as he noticed my cardboard floor mat and stopped. He looked around the room and stood there for what seemed like an eternity. Finally he shrugged his shoulders and left.

I taught myself to breathe again. I decided that if Majid wasn't here by dark I'd have to leave and take my chances, as slim as they might be. I sat in the back corner of the room and distracted myself, playing every tune I knew on my imaginary keyboard. I was lost in the third verse of Bob Marley's "Redemption Song" when the door creaked open again.

My knees nearly buckled with relief when I heard Majid whisper, "Reza? Reza, are you here?"

"I'm right here."

"I'm sorry I couldn't get back yesterday. You must be starving."

I looked inside the paper bag he handed me. The chunk of cheese and some loose nuts and dates looked like a feast.

"I got stuck yesterday. Two guards from the camp pulled in behind me as I arrived at the dump. I helped them search the truck." He laughed quietly. "Afterward we smelled as bad as you do. But then once I got back to camp I couldn't leave again. Abass wanted a repeat of the drinking session from the night before. I think he was hoping he could find out what happened to you, but no one seemed to know." He smiled the widest smile I'd ever seen on his friendly face.

"Is Ebi in trouble? Are any of the rest of them in trouble?"

"No. I don't think so. Once people realized you were gone, the guard who helped with the cans was questioned. He remembered talking to someone, but didn't remember Ebi. Some of the guards think all you boys look alike. I didn't volunteer any information, of course."

I felt like I'd been carrying around huge weights and could finally put them down. I took a bite of the hard cheese and had to force myself not to eat the whole piece in one gulp.

"So let's figure out what to do with you now. I have about an hour before I need to get back to camp. I brought you a change of clothes." He handed me a bundle. "The pants will be a bit big. They belong to my brother, but at least they don't smell or advertise you're on the run."

I stripped off the stiff canvas, eager to leave them hidden in this dingy little room. "Thank you, Majid. I . . . I can't thank you enough."

"The question is what to do next. You could hide in my brother's apartment, and I could try to drive you north tonight."

"No, Majid, you've done so much for me. I don't want to put you or anyone else in danger. If you can get me to a bus for Baghdad, you can leave me on my own." I sounded much braver than I felt.

"I suppose if we left straight away, I could get you to the outskirts of town, where you could catch the bus. But have you ever been in Baghdad before?"

"No, but I've been in Tehran plenty of times." I didn't mention that I'd always been with my parents or my uncle.

"What will you do there? It's a big city."

"If I got there today, Miles might still be at the Red Crescent office. Maybe he could set me up with some work or somewhere I could hide out for a while." Until I said this, I hadn't realized how every electron in my body wanted to see Miles before he left. Was Ebi right? Would I go with him if he asked? "He was planning on leaving today, right?" I asked, trying to keep desperation out of my voice.

"I think so. The major made it quite clear he was not welcome, and his visa was based on his work permit. If he's on the Red Crescent plane that usually comes in and leaves the same evening, he could have left last night, or might be going tomorrow night, or even tonight."

Majid stepped back and eyed me critically. "I suppose Baghdad is the best place for you. Even without papers you might be able to find something. Better than under Abass's eye anyway. Come, let's get to the truck." He handed me an old felt hat. "Wear this as well. Makes you look older."

Majid motioned me back as he opened the outside door. He looked up and down the street. "All right, into the cab, but slouch down in case you need to hide completely."

I climbed in and did as I was told. Majid pulled out into the flow of traffic. "Look in the glove box. I seem to remember a map of Baghdad in there. The Red Crescent office is in the Karrada neighborhood."

I rifled through papers and old rags in the glove box. I found a tattered map that looked like it was from a tourist brochure. "Here's a map, but most of the streets don't have names."

Majid ran his fingers through his hair. "It's a confusing city. The streets have numbers and the buildings have numbers, but many of the streets don't have names. You see the river there?"

"Yes." I traced my finger along the light blue line running through the center of the map.

"That's the Tigris, and it snakes through the whole city. If you can get yourself here"—he pointed to a place on the map where the river formed a peninsula of land—"that's where the Karrada neighborhood is. You can ask directions when you get there. But remember"—he smiled—"with your Arabic, don't do a lot of talking until you get somewhere safe."

"Thanks, I won't." I let a minute go by as I stole glances at the houses from under the hat. "I really appreciate this. I don't know why you're taking risks for me."

"I have two sons myself. They're eight and ten. I'm hoping this war is over before they are old enough to be sent to fight, but if they were captured I pray someone would show them some kindness."

"I hope so, too," I said.

Neither of us said anything else until we reached the outskirts of town. Majid pulled the truck over where a wooden sign marked a bus stop. He put his hand on my shoulder. "This is as far as I can take you. A bus to Baghdad comes along every few hours." He looked over his shoulder down the road. "If you're lucky there should be one soon. Standing here at the bus stop is too exposed. I would stand back in those trees until you see the bus coming."

Majid reached into his pocket and pulled out a few coins and a wrinkled bill. "This won't get you far, but at least you can pay for the bus to Baghdad." He glanced down the road again. "Who knows, when this is all done maybe I can find you. I'd like to come see you play music somewhere."

I didn't know what to do. I needed to get out of the truck, but I wanted to thank Majid. Shaking the guard's hand didn't seem like enough to show my gratitude.

Majid interrupted my thoughts. "Oh, I'm such a fool! I almost forgot." He reached around behind the seats and wrestled with something. "Here, help me, boy. It's the tar Miles left for you. I would have kicked myself if you'd left without it."

My eyes stung as I took the old leather case. I cleared my throat. "You've saved my life, Majid." I gave a short, strangled laugh. "I'll . . . I'll find you someday. I'll send you a tape." I jumped out of the truck before he could see my tears.

CHAPTER THIRTY-ONE

Majid pulled away and made a U-turn. He saluted as he headed back toward town and camp. I watched until the truck was at the horizon, then hurried back to the grove of trees as a car full of people pulled up to the stop.

It was cooler under the trees. I crouched behind a shrub where I was hidden but still had a view of the road. A father and three young boys tumbled out of the car. I listened to the boys' chatter. I wished I was part of their group, excited about my first trip to the city, my father's hand on my shoulder.

The sun was high in the sky. More people were dropped off; some talked, some stood by themselves and watched the long road. By the time ten people stood waiting, I thought it was safe to join the crowd. It couldn't be long before the bus arrived. But just as I was ready to leave my hiding place, a jeep carrying two soldiers came to a screeching halt. The crowd, as one, took an involuntary step back.

One of the soldiers got out of the car, eyeing everyone at the stop. I was glad for the Arabic Miles had taught. I heard the words *young, boy, thirteen, yellow pants.*

A thorn rubbed against my ankle, but I didn't dare move my leg. I was glad that Majid had thought to bring me a change of clothes.

The father of the young boys shook his head, motioning toward the group as he responded, his voice harsh.

The soldier walked very close to the man, until their noses were almost touching. In a loud voice he repeated his original question.

The youngest boy grabbed his father's leg and gave a small whimper. The man stepped back and bowed his head in the soldier's direction. He mumbled "Sorry" and some other words I didn't catch.

As the soldiers continued to question each and every person, I saw a bus on the horizon. In my mind I chanted, "Leave,

leave, leave." The soldier walked slowly around the group of people, pausing to watch the approaching bus as it got closer and began to slow down. I pulled myself farther back into the trees. Could I wait for the next bus? Should I run and try to find another way into town?

I let out breath as the jeep's driver waved to the other soldier and he climbed back into the car. The bus pulled into the cloud of dust left by the speeding jeep.

I took a step forward as the people at the stop were getting on the bus, the father and his boys first. A mother with a baby on her hip gathered her belongings and joined the end of the line.

My thoughts tumbled and tripped over each other. If I got on the bus now, would someone notice and report me? If I waited for the next bus, would they search that one, too? But if I took the next bus, I was pretty sure the Red Crescent office would be closed.

As the mother stepped onto the bus, I stopped thinking and ran to join the line, watching carefully how much the woman paid. I paid the same.

The driver didn't look twice at me. Nor did the other passengers as they settled their belongings for the long ride ahead. The baby, now on his mother's shoulder, dropped a little red truck. Instinctively I stooped to pick it up. The mother, hearing the toy drop, turned. Seeing me with the truck in my hand, she started chastising the young boy, then stopped in midsentence and looked straight into my face. In that second a dam broke somewhere in my body, sending adrenaline rushing through my veins. She knew something was different about me. I was sure of it. I forced myself not to look away. I returned her stare with as much of a smile as I could muster.

We reached an empty row. I slid in next to the window. I hunched as close to the glass as possible and fixed my gaze on the desert outside, feeling the woman and her child settling themselves in the seat across the aisle. After the bus started moving, I turned my head an inch to glance at them. The mother was rocking her child and staring in my direction.

She knows, I screamed at myself, the words reverberating around my head. How could I have been so dense as to pick up that stupid truck? I willed myself not to look back but just to relax. As I forced the fear from my body, I heard Ebi's voice. It was a young, bold Ebi, from the days when we stole figs in the marketplace. *Act like you belong, Maggot. Just act like you belong.*

At each stop, people got off and more people got on. The child fell asleep on the woman's lap. She stared out the window. Was she going to report me? Should I get off and try to catch another bus?

As I reached to take out the map Majid had given me, the bus swerved and slowed to a stop. People sat up, peering out the windows, asking questions. The doors of the bus opened and a soldier entered, a machine gun slung over his shoulder.

The flood of fear that had started to recede rushed back into every cell. Should I pretend to be asleep or pretend to be interested? If Ebi were here, we would be straining in our seats, watching every move. I tried to put on that face—the face I would wear if Ebi and I were together.

The man walked down the aisle, stopping at every row, looking at every face. He reached my row. His eyes settled on me.

He spoke in a gruff voice. I caught "travel" and "alone."

I thought of my accent, struggling to find enough words for a lie. But before I opened my mouth, the woman across the aisle spoke up.

"My son," were the only words I understood, but the woman motioned to me to sit next to her and held the baby out for me to hold.

I hoped my face didn't give away my surprise. The soldier watched as I climbed over and took the sleeping child. The soldier moved on to the next row. A moment later he walked back down the aisle and left.

I sat motionless. Holding the child felt awkward at first,

but after a few moments the baby shifted in his sleep, burrowing his downy dark hair into the crook of my arm.

I waited until the bus was under way again. Then I whispered in Arabic, "Thank you."

The woman reached into a bag on the floor and switched to Farsi. "I told him you were my son. Are you hungry?"

"I'm all right," I said, but the smell of fresh bread made my mouth water.

"Soldiers should have better things to do with their time than chase young boys." She handed me a hunk of soft, fresh bread with some meat stuffed in it and said, "Take this. It might be a while before you get food again. You were smart to ditch that awful yellow canvas uniform."

I stared at her. She smiled.

"I work in Camp Four. In the laundry. I wash and fold those terrible things."

I thought I'd just take a bite of the sandwich, but as soon as the food was in my mouth, I couldn't stop. It was the best thing I'd tasted in a year and a half. I ate the whole thing without taking a breath.

The woman laughed quietly and then whispered, "Better than onions and rice, yes? Where are you going?"

"To the Red Crescent office in the Karrada neighborhood."

"Get off with me. My stop is nearby. It won't take you long to walk."

I bowed my head and said quietly, "I don't know how to thank you."

She nodded and took the baby, who was starting to stir. "Less talking now. You don't exactly sound like my son will when he's your age."

I nodded back.

Later on, the landscape began to change. After the beige of the camps, I felt my brain flood with the colors of people's clothes, the small towns, then factories and warehouses piling on top of one another as we got closer to the city. I watched as the woman pointed out the window. The little boy, now awake, squealed and mimicked his mother. Soon we were in the city, with its large office and apartment buildings.

The woman leaned into me. "Our stop is next. Did you have a bag, too, or just the musical instrument?"

"Just the tar," I said. "I'll carry this bag for you." I picked up a small suitcase from under the seat.

I followed the woman off the bus. She put her bags down and began to readjust the baby in a sling on her hip.

I looked at the three bags at her feet. "Can I help you with this stuff?"

"No. Get on your way so you reach Karrada before dark. Offices usually close by five thirty."

I faced the direction the bus had gone. For a moment I wished I could climb into the sling with the little baby. It would be so easy to pretend this kind woman was my mother. Then I felt the weight of the tar in my hand and remembered Miles's applause when we'd played for the major.

"Yeah." I cleared my throat, making my voice deeper. "I should get going."

"Walk along this road, keeping the river to your left. You'll reach Karrada in about fifteen minutes. You'll have to ask when you get there. I don't know exactly where the office is, but watch who you ask. They probably aren't looking for you here, but there won't be many with your accent."

She smiled at me. I smiled back. I nodded and walked quickly in the direction she'd pointed. I wiped my eyes, amazed that my tears were so close to the surface, waiting to blur my vision at the slightest reminder of a family who could love me.

CHAPTER THIRTY-TWO

By the end of the block, I began to take in the bustle around me. I'd thought I was used to Arabic from hearing it in the camp, but the language all around me seemed fast and garbled. The street was full of cars, and people darted past me on the sidewalk. I straightened my shoulders and crossed the street. I wanted to see the river, to walk by the river.

It was odd having a possession again. Strange to feel the world around me, the world outside the dusty camp yard. Now that I was in Baghdad, I could walk as far as I could see without anyone stopping me. But the sight of the sun low in the sky brought me back to the moment. For the hundredth time, I wondered if Miles was gone already.

I picked up my pace, following the river. The map was no help. So many streets weren't listed. Without a watch I had to guess what time it was. Just as panic took hold of me, I noticed that the river had widened. Majid said I would find the Red Crescent office in the neighborhood where the river formed a peninsula of land. The water was slow moving, almost still. Upstream I thought I saw what could be a jut of land sticking into the river. I kept walking. The sun was disappearing behind buildings, and more and more people streamed out of offices on their way home.

At every street sign, I looked down at the map, trying to figure out where I was. I moved forward. It was almost like swimming in a sea of people.

I stopped suddenly, hearing two men speaking Farsi behind me.

"Excuse me, sir," I said to one of them. "I'm looking for the office of the Red Crescent."

A look of surprise passed over the man's face, but he said, "I know it's near here, but I'm not sure where."

I murmured a thank-you and scanned the crowd for

someone else who might speak my language. The man grabbed my sleeve.

"Wait, young man." He'd turned to the man next to him. "Izadi, this young man is looking for the Red Crescent office. It's near here, yes?"

"Yes." The man's eyes traveled from my disheveled hair to my shoes. "It's two blocks up and one to the right." He glanced at his watch. "I think they close at five thirty. That's ten minutes."

"Thanks." I crossed the street before either man could ask any questions. The next block was packed with people. I moved as fast as I could without actually running, dodging a young woman with a baby carriage and barely missing an old woman, her arms full of packages.

Finally I ran the last two blocks until I saw the familiar symbol hanging above a wooden door. I slowed down to catch my breath. The office had a large window in the front, and I could see several people inside. At last I was here, but what was I going to say? I hadn't figured it out and there wasn't time to now.

As I watched, I saw someone inside walk toward the door. I realized they might be coming to lock up. I needed to act quickly. When I opened the door, a short man with a mustache came toward me holding a ring full of keys. Behind the man were two other men packing briefcases at cluttered desks.

The man with the keys said something to me in Arabic. I caught the word "tomorrow."

"But I just wanted to ask a few . . ."

The man shook his head and switched to Farsi. "No, you must come back tomorrow. It is almost time for the call to prayer."

One of the other men walked up. My heart leaped as I realized it was Miles's friend Masood.

"Hey . . ." I started toward him in recognition, but Masood stopped me with a subtle shake of his head.

Masood spoke to the mustached man in Arabic, but I think he said, "I can take care of this if you want to go."

Looking at me, the older man said in Farsi, "I told the boy the office is closed, and I meant that the office is closed."

Masood looked at me and shrugged. He glanced around the office, then back at me with an apologetic smile. Before Masood turned away, he raised his eyebrows and mouthed the word "Tomorrow?" I tried to catch Masood's eye again, but the other man herded me out of the office.

I stood with my back to the office door. I heard the familiar notes of prayer float over the building tops. Men hurried by, anxious to get to prayer. I wanted to plead with Masood, but when I looked back inside the office, it was dark. My eyes stung with anger. I wanted to hit someone. I slumped against the building instead. Miles might still be in town, and I had no way of knowing.

Suddenly I heard a hiss to my right. It was Masood, motioning me over. "Sorry about my boss in there. Sometimes I think he forgets we work for an aid organization. Do I know you? Are you one of Miles's boys?"

I hesitated, worried for the first time that someone at the Red Crescent might turn me in and take me back. "I'm . . . my name . . . I'm Reza. I was—"

"You're that kid Miles was talking about. From Camp Six. We saw you there when we visited."

"That's me," I said. I tried to hide the rush I felt.

"What are you doing here, kid? Did you escape?"

I nodded.

Masood let out a whoosh of air. "Okay, that presents some challenges. You know Miles is gone." He glanced at his watch. "Or will be soon. I don't understand. How did you get here?"

"Once Miles left, one of the guards beat me up, started talking about killing me. I snuck out. I wanted . . ." I hesitated again, afraid to reveal my plan. But if I didn't do it now, it would be too late, so I let it come out in one breath. "I wanted to see Miles before he left."

Masood rocked back on his heels. "I don't know, kid. That'd be quite a risk for Miles, you being an escapee." Then Masood laughed, shaking his head. "What am I saying? Miles is all about risk."

Masood looked up and down the street. He shook his head and muttered something to himself.

I caught his eye. "Excuse me, sir. Did you say something?"

He laughed, reaching down to ruffle my hair. "I said I'm acting like a loon and my friend Miles is a sentimental sod. I should stay far away from his mayhem. But I rarely take my own advice." He reached in his pocket and pulled out a few wrinkled bills. "The government doesn't take too kindly to us helping escapees. Not good for you or me if I'm seen with you, but the airport is about fifteen minutes from here. The plane leaves in about an hour. It usually goes when the pilot's finished with dinner and he feels like going. Sometimes he goes early and leaves folks running down the tarmac.

"If you can find a cab, you might just get there in time to catch Miles. You can't miss the big white plane with the Red Crescent on the tail. Watch yourself. I bet that idiot will be happy to see you, but it won't be true of everyone. Come back tomorrow, and we'll try to help you."

I smiled and nodded.

"Head down to that corner." Masood pointed to the left.

"Then turn right. You'll come to a busy street where there's a taxi stand. Better move along. At this point you won't be able to get a taxi until prayers are over, but you'll want to be first in line if you can." Just then the side door of the building began to open.

"Go. If my boss sees you, we'll both be done for. Good luck. Tell Miles I expect to hear from him."

I waved over my shoulder as I ran to the corner. Once there I slowed down. I didn't want to call attention to myself. Running past a large group of men in prayer was not subtle.

I saw the taxi stand ten yards away. Two people were already waiting. As soon as prayers were done, the first man in line got into the waiting car. The man in front of me looked up and down the street for more taxis. I did, too. I tried to calculate how much time had passed since Masood and I had talked. How much time did I have before Miles's plane took off?

A second taxi came, and the man in front of me left. I shifted my weight from one foot to the other. At least five minutes passed. I silently chanted, *Come on, come on, come on.*

Finally an old taxi chugged up. I opened the squeaky back door and scrambled into the backseat, searching my brain for the right Arabic words. "Sir, do you speak Farsi?"

"A little," the driver mumbled.

"I need to get to the airport as soon as possible." I almost said "and step on it." It was a line from one of Ebi's favorite movies. Ebi would have loved the chance to say that. We would have laughed together, but now I could only muster a sad smile.

"Catching a plane?" grunted the driver.

"Uh . . . me?" I hadn't prepared a lie. "Uh . . . no. Someone from the Red Crescent office forgot his tar." I lifted the case. "They sent me to catch up with him if I can."

The driver shrugged and nodded.

The taxi sped through the city. The setting sun gave everything an amber clarity. I leaned against the backseat and closed my eyes.

As we went around a long curve in the road, the driver swore. I opened my eyes and saw a huge line of cars in front of us.

"Accident," said the driver as he slammed his hand on the steering wheel.

"Nooo." The word came from me like a howl.

"Nothing I can do."

"How far from here?" I asked.

"Three minutes."

It was almost completely dark. I wondered if I'd be able to tell if I saw Miles's plane take off overhead. The thought tightened my throat, making it hard to swallow.

Reaching into my pocket, I pulled out the wrinkled bills and handed them to the driver. I picked up the tar and opened the taxi door.

"You crazy? It's dark. Traffic. You'll break your neck."

I ran. And I kept running. My head went down to watch my feet and back up to see where I was going. I ran as fast as I'd ever run. The tar case banged against my leg. My lungs felt like I was breathing sand. But my focus was on running, on finding the white plane.

After minutes that seemed like hours, I saw the airport ahead. Seconds later I let out a yell. There, sitting on the tarmac, all its doors open, was a white plane. A red crescent was painted on the tail.

I ran to the chain-link fence and sank to my knees. I gulped huge mouthfuls of air. When my panting stopped, I realized that I needed a plan.

The plane wasn't far from the fence. It was low to the ground with a short flight of stairs in the front and in the back. It was different from the planes I'd seen in movies. It wasn't fancy. Through the windows I could see some seats, but it was mostly taken up with cargo: machinery, boxes, and luggage. Up front, I saw a few people moving around, stowing luggage. Did I see a flash of fiery hair? Near the back of the plane, at the bottom of the stairs, were a few large boxes waiting to be loaded.

Where I knelt, I was just out of the lighted zone on the tarmac. Ten meters away was an open gate in the fence. But a man with a clipboard stood near the gate, supervising the loading.

Another man in a dark uniform approached the gate, asking a question.

Clipboard man held up five fingers.

What did that mean? Five more boxes? Five minutes? I groaned to myself. What could I do? Then my eye caught the glint of something lying nearby—a broken bottle. I suddenly had a plan. It was a risky plan, maybe too risky. Maybe I should turn around and try to find my way in Baghdad.

Out of nowhere, I heard Uncle's voice . . . *I hope that sometime, somewhere, there'll be a place where you can grow your gift.* I felt his hand on my shoulder. Taking this risk might mean I could find that place Uncle believed in. This could be my chance to become the kind of man who could live in that place.

I waited until the guy loading boxes had hefted a huge package and entered the plane. I grabbed the shiny broken bottle at my feet. I lobbed it over the fence, right over the head of clipboard man. It skidded and shattered near the front of the plane. The minute the man looked toward the broken bottle, I ran through the gate and moved fast as a lizard to the opposite side of the plane. I crouched behind the large wheel.

The guy loading boxes came out of the plane. I couldn't understand what was said, but it was clear he'd heard the sound of breaking glass.

I couldn't believe my luck. Both men walked toward the broken glass. This left me a clear path into the back of the plane. I scrambled up the ramp into a large, dark compartment and ducked behind a stack of luggage, pulling the tar behind me. Thirty seconds later, the guy came in with the final load.

I was on the plane! I peeked from my hiding place. The front of the plane, where people sat in rows of four, two on either side of the aisle, was well lit. It was dark where I crouched, wedged between a huge box and a stack of suitcases. I sat with my knees drawn up almost to my chin. It would be impossible to stay this way for hours, but maybe I could move once the plane was off the ground.

From between two suitcases I saw a man in a jacket with a Red Crescent logo walk in and check the straps around the stack closest to where I sat.

I concentrated on staying completely still.

The man stuck his head out the door and said, "Okay, time to go." His Arabic was almost as bad as mine. Then he said it again in flawless Farsi, adding, "I want to get this bird in the sky." So this man was the pilot.

The man with the clipboard came in speaking Arabic, but switched to Farsi when he saw confusion on the pilot's face.

"Sir, did you see anyone on the tarmac as you got on board?

Someone threw a bottle and there shouldn't have been anyone near the plane."

"You sure it wasn't some drunk slumped against the building there?"

"We couldn't find anyone."

The pilot cursed and said, "All right, search the plane but be quick. I have breakfast plans in London."

The two men started jostling boxes and suitcases. It felt like my heart stopped beating. If I was caught there wasn't anything anyone could do. I'd be sent back to the camp or worse before I knew what hit me. I peered out on either side of me. To my right, the boxes were strapped securely to the bulkhead. To my left the stack of suitcases were strapped in, too, but maybe if I pushed I could hide myself.

With all my strength I shimmied between a stack of suitcases and the cold metal. Bolts from the bulkhead scraped my back. The tar case pinned my arm at a sharp angle. Even though my arm was healed, when it was stuck in this position, the pain made me want to scream. But I knew I couldn't make a sound. The two men were now standing right in front of me. The toe of my shoe was sticking out. If either of them looked down I was cooked.

My blood ran cold when I heard the words "behind" and "here." Then the pilot's voice said, "Come on, come on. There is nobody back here. Get off my plane and go search your other planes."

I didn't take a full breath until several minutes later when the big door slammed shut. With the slam, a terrible thought occurred to me. What if I'd gone through all this, gotten on this flight, and Miles wasn't here? Or what if Miles was on the plane and didn't want me?

These worries left my head a few minutes later when the plane started down the runway. I'd always imagined I'd look out the window during the first flight of my life, but here I was stuck behind luggage. The pilot's voice came over the loud-speaker, reminding the passengers in three languages to put on their seatbelts. I braced myself against the cold metal wall.

The plane moved faster than I expected, and then the nose of the big machine lifted into the air. Even tied down, the boxes and suitcases slid toward the back of the plane. It took all my strength to stay in place.

To keep my mind from spinning into what might go wrong, I silently sang "A Hundred Rubies," my favorite nursery rhyme when I was little. After a while the plane leveled off. I wriggled back to the space where I'd been sitting before. It felt odd. I knew we were moving fast, but now it hardly felt like we were moving at all. Once the blood was flowing in my limbs again, I risked a better look at the passengers.

And there was Miles's unmistakable red head. When I saw him a few rows from the back, I took my first deep breath in ages. Even better, the seat next to him was empty.

My feet were ready to leap the distance between the boxes and Miles, but something stopped me. Maybe it was the fear that Miles wouldn't want me here. Maybe it was that I wanted to feel more distance from the camp. I waited, but when my legs started to fall asleep, I decided it was time.

Slowly I stood up, reminding myself to act as if I belonged. I walked up to the empty seat. Miles's face looked drawn and paler than usual. His arms were folded over his chest. He stared into the black of the tiny window. I cleared my throat. "Excuse me, anyone sitting here?" Miles sighed, barely turning his head. "No, no, it's empty. Make yourself—"

Miles stopped as his eyes connected with the tar. His gaze trailed up until our eyes locked. A smile took root and spread across his face. I felt a matching grin stretch from ear to ear.

"Rez." It looked like he wanted to say more, but I was going to make him wait.

"You told me to get on a plane and visit. Is this too soon?"

Miles pulled me down into the seat. We looked at each other for a long time.

"Lord Almighty. It's going to take some fancy work to figure out what to do with you, Reza. If I weren't so happy to see you,

I'd hit you over the head." His grin got even wider. "But I am very, very happy to see you."

My hand rested on the tar case. Miles covered my hand with his. For a while we just smiled. Then we both looked out the window. We watched the plane's wing, its light flashing through the black night. I didn't know exactly where this trip would end, but I knew it would be a place where songs would be sung.

AUTHOR'S NOTE

This is a work of fiction. While historical and political events are depicted as close to reality as possible, all the characters are entirely of my imagination. It is important to note that, unlike Reza, most of the boys who landed in POW camps in Iraq in the 1980s spent the majority of their teenage years there.

National Public Radio's *Fresh Air* host Terry Gross planted the seeds of this book in a 2005 interview with the author P. W. Singer about his book *Children at War*. His discussion of what happened to a generation of Iranian boys took only a few minutes of the interview, but I couldn't stop thinking about it. My first thought was, *Someone needs to tell this story from the boys' perspective.* My second thought was, *That someone is not me.*

I am not a thirteen-year-old boy. I am not Muslim. I've never been to Iran or Iraq. Yet the story wouldn't let me go. I found myself researching what happened to these young boys. I read the wonderful graphic novel *Persepolis* by Marjane Satrapi, which portrays this period from a young girl's perspective, but a boy's story had not been told. I was certain that it should be.

As preoccupied as I was, I had misgivings about telling a story so outside my personal experience. Two sources gave me the confidence to start writing, and for them I am eternally grateful. *Children at War* referenced a book called *Khomeini's Forgotten Sons: The Story of Iran's Boy Soldiers,* written by Ian Brown, an aid worker who taught in the Iraqi POW camps in the 1980s. Mr. Brown graciously allowed me to use his extensive nonfiction accounts to bring my characters alive. Eventually he critiqued my manuscript and offered invaluable feedback. My character, Miles, is not Ian, but if they met on some planet where fictional characters exist, I hope they would be friends.

My second source was a neighbor, Masood Moghaddam. I discovered that Masood came to the United States at thirteen so that he, unlike my character Reza, could avoid being sent to war. Masood's memories of growing up in Iran and how his life changed after the revolution enriched this story immeasurably.

I did all I could to learn about this turbulent period. Detailed information is limited, and given the nature of the subject and the volatility of the times, the facts are not always clear. In several cases even firsthand accounts differed. I searched and sifted—doing my best to get to the heart of the story. I am extremely grateful to a number of Iranian readers, in particular

Banafsheh Keynoush, who carefully read and commented on my work. To a person other experts were helpful and supportive; due to historic and current connections, however, they have asked to remain anonymous.

I've always been interested in the journey we take from the religious ideas and practices of our parents to owning our own beliefs. For boys like Reza, this coming-of-age experience was tangled with war. I tried to do justice to their story.

ACKNOWLEDGMENTS

As described in the Author's Note, I couldn't have written this book without the help of several generous people with firsthand experience. I could also fill pages thanking Lin Oliver and the Society of Children's Book Writers and Illustrators (SCBWI). Lin critiqued this story in its infancy and declared herself its godmother. She has been true to that title, offering support and sage advice. Over the years SCBWI has schooled me in the art and craft of writing through its wonderful conferences and online support. In 2014 I was lucky enough to be awarded an SCBWI Work-in-Progress grant that brought this manuscript some critical attention. Just as important, through SCBWI I've found an incredibly supportive writing community. There are not enough pages here for me to name you all, but please know you are loved—particularly the wild YAMS crew and the Better Books Marin alumni. Even a thesaurus couldn't provide the words to describe the gratitude and love I have for my longtime critique group—M'Ladies of the

Book—Alison Berka, Amanda Conran, Lisa Schulman, and Elizabeth Shreeve. Likewise for our newest member Shannon Ledger, best beta reader and friend a girl could have. Also thanks to our local bookstore—our second home—Book Passage in Corte Madera, California.

This book and my writing were made better by Emma Dryden's red pen and warm friendship. The book would truly not be in your hands without my extraordinary agent, Erin Murphy. Erin's love of children's lit and the magical gang she gathers around her make the world a better place. Erin brought me to the wise and clever Sally Doherty. Sally, Christian Trimmer, Rachel Murray, and all the fabulous folk at Henry Holt believed in this story that others had not quite known what to do with. A special shout-out to Rich Deas, who created the beautiful cover.

Huge thanks to my magnificent and far-flung family—siblings, cousins, aunts, and uncles. All have supported me since day one. Particular thanks to Dad (my earliest and dearest editor), Mom, Eli, Amanda, Mindy, and Evelyn, who all read first drafts and remembered my characters as if they were friends. My nephew Ben Joseph has lived for music since the day he was born, and he helped me understand what mattered to Reza. Finally, to David and Martha—I am so much better because of you and thank my lucky stars every single day that you are my galaxy.